MY DAY A̲

"Intriguing and wildly entertaining. The push-pull dynamic between Beth and Regan is riveting and enthralling. Urban's prose is lovely and easily readable, and Beth and Regan are captivating. Refreshing and memorable."

—The BookLife Prize

"A bittersweet story of two women wanting more. Fans of Jude Deveraux's *The Summerhouse* will be delighted by the body and life swap-for-a-day story of middle-aged mom Beth Barony and young super starlet Regan Forrester. A satisfying, page-turning summer read!"
–Teresa LaBella, author of the New Life in Love series

"The phrase 'be careful what you wish for takes on new meaning in *My Day As Regan Forrester*. Urban takes the impossible and makes it probable, with humor and a dash of emotional heft. Poignant, fast-paced, and funny."
–Elaine L. Orr, author of the Jolie Gentil mysteries

"A great escape that leaves you content with your return . . . Urban balances weight and whimsy in an entertaining plot with characters you care about and root for. A great anytime read!"
– Joanne Salemink, author of *Scout's Honor*

Praise for Misty Urban

"Urban allows readers to peek into the lives of fictional individuals that seem so real they could be your friend or neighbor or even an aspect of yourself."
—Jodie Toohey, Legacy Book Press

"A keen observer of the human condition, a skillful wordsmith who writes with powerful clarity, and an absorbing storyteller who commands your attention."
—X.H. Collins, author of *Flowing Water, Falling Flowers*

Also by Misty Urban

FICTION

A Lesson in Manners: Stories

The Necessaries: Stories

Married, Living in Italy: Stories

SCHOLARSHIP

Monstrous Women in Middle English Romance

Melusine's Footprint:
Tracing the Legacy of a Medieval Myth

FEATURED COLLECTIONS

Sisters: An Anthology

DOMESTIC: An Anthology

Roswell: A Literary Collection

My Caesarean: 21 Mothers on the C-Section
Experience and After

These Interesting Times: Surviving 2020 in the Q-C

MY DAY AS REGAN FORRESTER

MISTY URBAN

Canty Dames

Published by Canty Dames
Muscatine, IA
www.cantydames.com

Copyright © 2021 by Misty Urban
All rights reserved

Cover images licensed from Adobe Stock
with elements from Freepik.com and Vecteezy.com
Cover design by Jessica Kiefer
Book design © 2017 BookTemplates.com
All rights reserved

This is a work of fiction. All characters, incidents, and events
are products of the author's imagination or are used
fictitiously with no relation to actual persons or events.

ISBN-13: 978-1-7362247-2-4

My Day as Regan Forrester/Misty Urban—1st ed.
Printed in the United States of America
Subject: Fiction/Fantasy/Contemporary

10 9 8 7 6 5 4 3 2 1

MY DAY
AS
REGAN
FORRESTER

MISTY URBAN

TABLE OF CONTENTS

To anyone who's maybe, sometimes, just a little bit

wondered about a different life

1 • THE WISH

Beth Barony spent her forty-second birthday exactly as she wanted to.

And when she woke up the next day, she was someone else.

As she lived it, the day didn't seem extraordinary. The kids were at their respective camps and the summer honors class Beth taught didn't meet on Fridays. Her husband refused to take the day off, but that was no surprise. Only hospitalization or cataclysm could lure Daniel Barony away from the law office when he was wrapping a big case.

Beth told herself she was used to it. She spent the day at the spa with her best friends, Joan and Sherice. After manicures, pedicures, and facials, they smuggled bottles of mimosas into the movie theater with the reclining seats and watched a matinee showing of the latest blockbuster, blow-'em-up, world-ending alien invasion movie.

Halfway through another endless action sequence Joan leaned over and whispered, "Let's go get a cocktail" and they went to their favorite restaurant, found a table near the wood-burning oven, and ordered a pitcher of Bellinis.

"Forty-two will be the best year yet," Joan declared, filling Beth's glass. "You know how you wake up at thirty with that feeling of, oh my God, thank goodness the crap about finding myself is finally over? Every year of your forties is less crap. It's great. You'll see."

Beth opened her mouth to agree and was surprised by what came out.

"Do you feel like you're living the life you're supposed to be living?" she blurted, then hid behind her glass as her friends stared. "I mean," she said in a small voice, "do you?"

Sherice leaned forward, chin on her fist. She'd thrown her hair into a colorful wrap and wore all the jewelry she couldn't wear on the pediatric floor, big gold hoops and a chunky necklace that caught the light. "What's wrong, honey?"

"Nothing." Beth twirled the stem of her glass. "Everything's fine. Just as it should be." She forced a smile. "I'm the luckiest girl alive. I know that."

Joan, wearing a tailored blouse and slacks even on her casual day, tapped her manicured fingers on the polished table. "Have you made your birthday wish?"

Beth stared into her glass. The birthday wish was her custom, one she'd let Joan and Sherice in on ages ago. Every birthday she set her sights on a new goal she wanted to accomplish, a dream she wanted to come true. But this year . . .

"I have no idea what to wish for," Beth admitted. "Is that sad?"

"I wish I could be thin like Joan," Sherice volunteered.

"We all wish we could be as thin as Joan," Beth said, comparing her comfortable, average-sized body to their slender friend.

"And I wish I had you two's gorgeous curves." Joan lifted her glass in a toast.

"I wish I were as smart as Beth," Sherice said after a long sip.

"Sweetheart, nobody's as smart as Beth," Joan answered.

"Tell me this," Sherice said. "If you had a do-over, what would you change?"

"Say what?" Joan's perfectly arched, darkened brows flew up her forehead. "Of all of us, Beth is the one who has it together. She's got the man, healthy kids—" She turned to Beth. "You love your job. Your house. Your kids. And Barony. Right?"

The prosecco was making Beth queasy. She rarely drank this much.

"I do." Beth nodded. She met Barony in their first year of college and they were friends before they dated and married right out of grad school. She still called him Barony, since only his mom called him Daniel, and he'd been a solid and faithful husband for eighteen years.

"I love our house," Beth went on. "The kids have never given us a minute of trouble. I love my job at the school. And it feels like . . . " She trailed off. "There's nothing left to wish for. The rest of my life is going to look exactly like this, going to school and then coming home, paying the bills and trying to hide the grey hair."

Joan slurped her Bellini. "And that's bad?"

"No! That's why I feel guilty for even saying anything. I have nothing to complain about." She should just shut up. Sherice was a pediatric nurse single parenting two children, a boy who was on the autism spectrum and a girl who was gender questioning. Sherice loved her kids fiercely—so did Joan and Beth—but there were plenty of struggles.

Joan was single after a painful marriage marked by infertility, abuse, and a messy divorce. She ran the domestic violence shelter and poured her energy into helping women and children get out of danger into safety and self-sufficiency. Beth's friends did work that made a difference in people's lives every day.

Beth, meanwhile, taught literature to talented high achievers at the International School, fixed lunches for her kids and ran them to practices, made dinner every night and cleaned up after, and then fell into bed with a book. She spent her weekends at sports meets and music recitals, made a big dinner every holiday, once a year booked a family vacation to somewhere fun. And that was the scope of her life.

"It's just that when I look at you two—what you do every day, how much it matters—I ask myself if I'm doing what I should be doing. I'm not unhappy. But I feel like I'm not really *in* my life. Something's missing. It's like—" Beth paused. "Maybe I'm supposed to be doing something else. *Be* somewhere else."

"Is this a mid-life crisis?" Joan swirled the liquid in her glass. "Are you going to ditch Barony and the kids and run away to travel the world? Because if you do, I want to come with you."

Beth responded with a shaky laugh.

"I'd love to do that, right now," she said honestly, "and there's absolutely no chance that I will."

"It's perimenopause," Sherice said. When Beth cried out in protest, her friend nodded in emphasis. "Mmm-hmm. The hormones are starting, girl. First you feel itchy, then you can't sleep, then the hot flashes. I'm sorry, but that's how it goes."

"I think it's that movie," Joan announced, reaching for the pitcher. "We should have picked the chick flick about the book club. Instead we go to the superhero movie with that hard-bodied little Hollywood princess—what's her name again? She's on the cover of every magazine I look at these days."

"Regan Forrester," Beth replied. When Joan's brows rose again, she explained. "My students love her. But I don't think this is about her. I mean, I never looked like that even when I was twenty-four."

"But she's a huge celebrity," Sherice said. "And you're feeling invisible right now. You wonder what it would be like to have people notice you. Pay attention to you."

"Invisible?" Beth said, startled. "I didn't think of it that way. Maybe I am a little jealous. I don't have that kind of talent."

"Everybody has a talent," Joan insisted. "And I wouldn't say her life is so wonderful. Didn't you read that interview in *People*?"

"Um, no," Sherice said. "Because I do not subscribe to *People*, and I don't have time to read it if I did, and I certainly don't want to hear some teeny Hollywood princess complaining how hard it is to be rich and gorgeous."

"She seemed kind of sad."

Joan twirled the ends of her silk scarf. "She talked about how her mom got her into acting when she was six, and she's never done anything else. And how she doesn't have any real friends, at least not girlfriends, because Hollywood is so bitchy and competitive. She basically said her whole life is her boyfriend, though the way she talks about him creeps me out, about how they're soulmates and such, when he's a has-been who's at least fifteen years older than she is and only using her to get attention."

Beth sipped her Bellini. Her nose tingled. "No girlfriends? That is sad. I don't know what I would do without you two. I would cease to exist."

"Amen, sister." Sherice raised her glass and the three of them toasted with a musical clink. The light from the overhead chandelier flashed through Beth's glass, winking at her.

"See, Beth?" Joan said. "Nobody's life is perfect. Even the people who seem to have it figured out don't, not really. You never really know what's going on inside."

"You just need some excitement, girl," Sherice said with a wink. "See if Barony can do something about that, huh?"

"Maybe when he wins the case he's working on, he'll remember he has a wife." They clinked glasses in another toast, and Beth let the conversation move on. But the nagging, hollow feeling persisted, as it had for months now, perhaps years.

She thought about it as she drove home to the empty house. With the kids gone she got to have everything as she liked it, tidy, clear, every item in place. Quiet and a bit—boring. No clutter. Nothing dramatic. No surprises.

She thought about it as she dressed for dinner. *Excitement.* When was the last time something had stretched her? Exhilarated her? Made her feel recklessly, gloriously alive? She'd spent twenty years of her life working to build a stable home, financial security, solid relationships with people she loved, and now she wanted more? What more was there?

She pulled on the new dress she'd bought shopping with Joan last weekend and tried a new style on her hair. Barony came home from work and greeted her with a kiss, then drove them to the steakhouse where they'd had their anniversary dinner for the last eighteen years. They talked about her classes, his cases, and what the kids were doing as she nibbled at her salmon and Barony wolfed his steak. And she was startled to look across the table and realize that her husband had become nearly a stranger.

How was that even possible? This was the life she and Barony had dreamed of, wanted, built together. But she'd been going on so long in the same routine that she couldn't say quite how she'd gotten here.

Why did it feel like she wasn't really *in* her life? The tracks had been laid so well, so firmly, that she could step out of her life, run away like Joan had said, and everything would simply keep on churning without her.

She set down her wine glass. Barony liked a nice

merlot with his steak, but her head was still floating from all the champagne that afternoon.

"What do you think of my hair?" she asked, cupping the curls it had taken hours to create.

He gave her a cautious, you-must-be-testing-me look. "Did you change it?"

She sighed and pulled the wine glass toward her. "Nope."

"Well, I'm glad you're one of those women who doesn't mind going grey. I think hair dye always looks fake. The assistant from the law firm on this Cates case . . ."

Beth pushed away the tiny flare of resentment. She would have been surprised, frankly, if Barony picked up on her mood. He wasn't the most perceptive of men, at least not where his wife was concerned. They finished the bottle of red wine while soft music played overhead and the crowd turned from families to older couples. At home they swirled in the Jacuzzi on their new back porch and then had sex the same way they'd been having sex since their daughter Abby was born.

Barony fell asleep at once and Beth lay looking out the window at a hazy full moon. She still hadn't made her birthday wish.

Because she couldn't bring herself to say what she wished for. It felt like a betrayal of everyone she loved to form the words, even in her head.

On the edge of sleep, images from the movie tumbled into her head: the beautiful actress in a skin-tight bodysuit, fighting off alien invaders, saving the world, and then telling interested reporters that she simply didn't know what else to do with her life, since she'd never known anything else.

She felt sorry for the girl, so sad, so lost. Still, Beth thought as she slipped beneath the surface of sleep, it must be easier to try new things when you're young and gorgeous and famous and rich. Slip away . . . shed your skin . . . reinvent yourself into something new entirely . . .

Then she woke up to find that, somehow, she'd done just that.

2 • THE AWAKENING

Beth stared at the canopy above her bed. Since when did she have a purple princess canopy above her bed?

It was a pretty, gauzy lavender color, like looking at the underside of clouds. It was something she might have loved when she was fourteen, although her daughter, twelve, would laugh herself silly if Beth suggested something like that for her décor.

She must have had an awful lot of wine, except her body felt wonderful. She felt strong and healthy with not a sore spot anywhere, like she was twenty years old again.

She sat up, but she had to be dreaming.

That wasn't the nightstand from the bedroom set she'd made Barony buy for their fifteenth wedding anniversary. The lamp had a pink scarf draped around it with dangling strings of beads. There was a bottle of lotion, but it wasn't the lotion she put on her feet right before bed.

Her annotated copy of *Wuthering Heights* was missing, and that wasn't her cell phone. She'd had the same old beat-up phone for going on three years. This contraption on her nightstand, quietly vibrating as it registered an incoming text, was thin, unscratched, a much more sophisticated piece of equipment, and it was a bright plum purple.

Beth pushed back the covers of the bed. She was still in her negligee—her birthday present to her husband—but it was a lot tinier than she remembered, with more see-through lace. Beth glanced down at herself and did a double take. Wow, the light was especially forgiving this morning. Her legs looked lean and long and tanned, not a trace of cellulite. She couldn't even see the scar from the bicycling accident five years ago.

Her belly looked firm and flat, too, and her boobs—no wonder Barony had given her extra attention last night. Maybe she should suggest a morning reenactment, Beth thought with a smile. Her body felt amazing, lithe and strong and full of energy. She couldn't remember the last time she'd woke up feeling this good. Barony was definitely in trouble, she thought as she turned to wake him up.

She screamed.

"What? What? What?" The man in her bed who was most definitely *not* Barony startled awake, arms flailing. "Someone breaking in?"

Beth clapped her hands to her mouth. "How did you get here?" she cried.

He shook his head. "Jesus. Give me a heart attack." He ran a hand over his shaved head and stubbled chin. "I got in late. You were already in bed."

He looked like an actor on a show Beth used to watch in high school. The weirdness of this kept her still for a moment. "What did you do with Barony?"

"With who?" His eyebrows snapped together in a frown.

"With Barony!" Beth shrilled. "My husband!"

"Your *what*?" He sat up and swung around in the bed, grabbing her wrist.

"Where is my house?" Beth looked around the room. "Where is my bedroom? Where is my life?"

He grabbed her by both arms and looked her over. "Damn it, Regan! What did you take?"

"I didn't take anything! I went to sleep in my own bed and I woke up here! Who's Regan?"

He shook her, and her head bobbed back and forth, which cut off the scream rising in her throat. "Benny gave you some shit again, didn't he! And you took it. When you know it makes you all paranoid and freaky."

"What on earth did he give me?" Beth gasped.

"Hell if I know!" He held both her wrists in one hand and looked around the room, muttering. "I'm going to kill Benny this time—"

"Don't kill him before he can make it stop!" Beth took a deep breath. *Don't panic, Beth.* She was a rational person. There had to be a rational explanation for this.

"Relax, babe. You're just going to have to chill until it's over."

"Let's make it over now!" Beth said. "I have to get home to my husband, and my job, and I'm supposed to teach *Wuthering Heights* to the summer honors class next week." She shook her wrists. "Let go of me!"

He drew back a hand, and Beth's jaw dropped. When she said nothing, his hand dropped as well.

She yanked her arms out of his grasp. "Were you about to *hit* me?"

"Listen to yourself! You sound like a crazy bitch."

"Well, I *feel* like a crazy bitch," Beth shouted.

"This is not my room, I have no idea how I got here, and—" She glanced down at the cleavage exposed by the negligee. "This is not my body. What the hell happened last night?"

"Look at me." He leaned forward, so close that she had no choice. "Now listen. You freak out every time Benny gives you something. I don't know why you keep pulling this, Regan! Seriously, I ought to—"

"Who is *Regan*?" Beth choked.

"You." He spoke over her, taking her wrists once more. "Are Regan Forrester. We live in West Hollywood. You're twenty-four years old and a movie star who is—" his eyes ran over her— "hot as all hell, though you are crazy as a chigger."

I—" he shook her wrists again—"am your boyfriend. This is our apartment. Well, your apartment. Benny gave you something, and that's why you're having this weird freak out. You need to go back to bed and sleep it off. And stop looking at me like that. You're giving me the creeps."

"You have the creeps?" Beth repeated. "You are? *I'm* having a psychotic break. I need to call Sherice. Or Joan. And find Barony." Her volume escalated.

He shook his head and tossed her wrists away. "You better take an aspirin and lie down. I'll—" He looked at her, frowning.

"Don't you dare hit me!" Beth snapped. "No one has ever hit me in my life."

He laughed. "Wouldn't your mama love to hear that? Give me your phone," he demanded as the device trilled a musical tone. "That's probably

Benny texting to see if he killed you."

Beth held the phone to her chest out of some wild, reflexive sense of self-preservation. "I'm calm. I need to think. Go away, please."

He gave her a suspicious look, his eyes lingering on the negligee. "I'm gonna shower. And when I come out, you're going to be over this little freak out. Okay?"

"Yes. Okay. You do that." Beth watched as he walked into the bathroom, and then she stared at the back of the door and her reflection in the full-length mirror.

He wasn't kidding. By whatever trick of the light or consequence of the mind-melding drugs she had supposedly taken, she looked exactly like Regan Forrester.

Beth looked at the stylish smartphone. A picture of Regan Forrester and the man who had just started the shower stared back at her, both grinning. She looked at her hands. Her fingertips were long and painted scarlet, a color Beth would never wear because it washed out her skin.

There was a tattoo of a butterfly on the inside of one wrist. She was wearing a ring on her right hand that Beth had never seen before. Her wedding ring was missing.

She pinched her arm, hard, above the butterfly. Nothing happened except pain.

Nope, not dreaming.

What had *happened* to her last night? Had Joan and Sherice put something in the Bellinis?

No, they'd never do anything to hurt her. What

about the wine she'd shared with Barony? Had she gotten out of bed and gone somewhere after he fell asleep? Had she gone to some club and taken some drug that made her hallucinate? If she'd had a one-night stand, Barony would never forgive her. She would never forgive herself.

Slowly, because her red-tipped fingers were shaking, Beth punched a number into the phone and hit the green button.

* * *

When she was in grade school, Beth had a recurring dream that she was with her parents on the observation deck at the top of a very tall building, like the Space Needle in Seattle. She stood near the glass, looking down hundreds of feet, clinging to the legs of a woman she assumed was her mother.

But suddenly, in the dream, Beth saw her mother on the street below, her features very clear and magnified, her expression intent on something in front of her. Beth called out as loudly as she could, but her mother didn't turn or hear her, instead kept walking steadily away.

In panic, Beth turned to look at the face of the woman whose legs she was holding and saw a total stranger. In the dream she screamed and let go of the stranger's legs and then the glass disappeared and she was falling, falling through the air, still screaming, waiting for her mother to see her and grab her and bring her safely to the ground. She felt much the same way now, waiting for the call to connect.

The phone rang, then clicked, and then a sleepy voice said, "Who is this?"

The voice sounded familiar, but she couldn't place it. "Who is *this*?"

"Regan," the voice slurred. "Regan Forrester." The voice became a hint sharper, something about it vaguely recognizable. "Wait a minute—*who* is this?"

Beth almost laughed. If she was talking to Regan Forrester on the phone, then she couldn't somehow be in Regan Forrester's body. It was all some weird sort of delusion, just as the TV actor said. Maybe she had been taking drugs.

But she didn't laugh because something new occurred to her. "This is Beth Barony. What are you doing answering my phone?"

Some indistinguishable muttering followed. Beth worked hard to place the voice. She was sure she knew it, yet it sounded strange. She heard silence, some rustling, a bang that sounded like a bathroom door closing, and then, in an awed tone, "Holy shit. I didn't think it would actually *work*."

Recognition slapped her in the face. It was her voice. She was talking to a woman who was speaking to her in Beth's own voice.

"You didn't think *what* would actually work?"

A laugh followed, one that left no doubt in her mind. She had heard that laugh thousands of times, coming from her own mouth. "If you're Regan Forrester, what are you doing with my phone?"

"I think I'm in your house! What did you say your name was?"

Beth clutched the phone as if she could channel herself through the connection and wind up in the place she was supposed to be. "Beth Barony."

"Are you, um, do you have brown hair? You're short, and a little—hmmm? Forty-five, fifty?"

"Give me a break!" Beth yelped. "I just had a facial! I'm only forty-two. At my physical my doctor said I have the bloodwork of a woman half my age." She was proud of that.

"Whoops, sorry." Another chuckle. "Hey, I like this picture you have in your bathroom. I've thought about buying that picture. This is so weird."

"Weird doesn't begin to describe it." Beth closed her eyes. "I'm guessing you're in my body, Regan Forrester, because I seem to have woken up in yours."

"I'm really hot, aren't I?" Regan Forrester said.

3 • THE CALL

The bathroom door flew open and the TV actor glared at her. "Who are you talking to?"

"No one," Beth said, covering the phone with her hand.

"Is that Benny? Come here." He grabbed her wrist and yelled into the phone. "Benny, what shit did you give her? I'm gonna find you, and I'm gonna kick your ass!"

"Where are you going?" Beth watched as he swiped up a shirt, a set of keys, and his own phone.

"Out." She heard some stomping, then the slam of an outer door.

"That's your boyfriend?" Beth said into the phone.

"Yeah. Sexy, huh?"

"Does he yell at you a lot? He seems to have some aggressive tendencies, and he uses a lot of foul language. I actually thought he was going to hit me."

"Yeah, he's taking anger management classes. Court-ordered. I don't know that they're doing him any good."

Suddenly realizing Regan Forrester stood in her master bathroom, in her body—she still couldn't wrap her mind around that, somehow—Beth broke into a cold sweat. "Where's Barony?"

"Who?"

"My husband, Barony."

"What does he look like?"

"There's a picture of us in the bedroom."

It was a portrait from their wedding, an outdoor shot, taken beneath a tree on golf course of the country club where they'd had their reception. Beth's hair was flying in the breeze. Barony's smile was deep and whole and satisfied.

"Oh, wow. He's handsome."

Stay away from him, Beth almost said. She didn't have a chance if Regan Forrester made a play for her husband—but wait a minute. Regan was in her body. She was in Regan's.

Beth sat down on the bed, pressing a hand to her head.

"Tell me again how this happened."

"I don't know." Her voice sounded far away. "Whoa, are these your—do you have kids?"

"Yes. Drew and Abby. They're at camp right now." Which was great luck, because hopefully she could get home before her husband or children found out that their wife and mother had disappeared and left another person wearing her body.

"Aww. They're cute." A pause. "They were really cute babies, anyway."

"They're still cute," Beth snapped. Drew, seventeen, was gangly and awkward and fighting a tendency for breakouts. Abby, twelve, had braces and insisted on wearing really big glasses despite all Beth did to try to convince her to wear smaller frames.

"You said something worked. What worked?"

"Hey, you have a really nice house. Is this whole thing yours?" Regan said.

"Yes. Thank you. Regan, please tell me. What exactly did you do?"

"Well." A long silence followed. Beth pulled a pillow into her lap and squeezed it against her stomach, waiting. How long had it been since she'd had a firm, flat stomach? Not since her kids were born, that was for sure.

"I don't know, exactly, because the whole thing was really weird, and I was kind of out of it. But the idea was that I wished for a different life?"

"Excuse me?" Beth looked at the room around her. The bedroom was small, the narrow blinds closed against the sounds of street traffic and shouting voices, with a sheer fuchsia curtain draped across it. She could smell exhaust and possibly garbage from the street outside.

The décor wasn't anything to envy, mostly posters of movies and musicians she'd never heard of. Piles of clothes, gadgets, and junk covered the floors; a chair in the corner was piled high with fabric and shoes and what looked like a pair of evening gloves. There was a tall bureau with drawers hanging open and contents partially spilling out.

A vanity table stood cluttered with all sorts of bottles and jars, next to a tiny bookshelf crammed with shoes. It was chaotic and dusty, the kind of mess Beth wouldn't have tolerated even when she was a teenager.

Yet Regan Forrester was a movie star. She'd been in a blockbuster movie and there was talk of a sequel. Just this month Beth had seen her on the cover of three different magazines. What was she doing living in a crummy apartment?

"What do you mean, you wished for a different life?"

"I don't know. I was just feeling—you know, sad. So I did a spell. Seriously, this is your house? It is so nice! This is just the kind of thing I'm saving up to buy. All the places in Malibu are so expensive."

"We just finished the addition, so that added to the square footage," Beth said automatically. "Also the mortgage. But we really like it, and it's big enough for the kids."

She approached the vanity table and amid the clutter she saw a circle of candles and a shiny plate in the middle piled with ashes and a half-burned piece of paper. The pungent smell of burned herbs pricked at her eyes as she bent close to sniff.

"Where are you?" Beth asked, hearing a door open and close.

"I'm at your front door. I really love your house. Is that your neighbor? Hi!" Regan chirped, then whispered to Beth, "I'm waving at your neighbor. I don't see your husband anywhere, though."

"He's probably at work. Is his briefcase on the kitchen counter? I always ask him to put it in his office, but he always puts it on the kitchen counter. It drives me nuts."

"Just a minute. No, I don't see a briefcase. Is this the door to the garage?" A pause, and then, "I only see one car here. A Volvo? Really?" She giggled.

"Hey," Beth said. "I love that car." She smacked her hand to her forehead. "Focus! We have to focus here. I have lunch today with the dean, the credit card bill is due, and Joan and I have our exercise class this afternoon. This is not good. Regan—what kind of spell?"

"I don't know. He told me some things to do, so I did them."

A squeal of excitement pierced her ears, and Beth jumped. "What's the matter?"

"Look at all the food in your refrigerator! Are you a chef?"

Beth swallowed an irrational laugh. Nothing about this situation made any sense. "Hardly. Regan, please. We have to make this go back. I have to get ready for school."

"You're still in school? Aren't you a little old for that?"

"I'm a teacher," Beth said, annoyed. "I'm teaching a summer class to a group of honors students. I'm supposed to meet with the dean today to—"

Her throat closed. She had asked for a meeting because, frankly, the class was not going well. She sensed her students were about to revolt from boredom. She could not meet her dean like this.

"Oh, hello kitty," Regan cooed. "Does kitty want his breakfast? You're certainly a big, fluffy kitty, aren't you?"

"That's Chester," Beth said, hearing the yowls. "His food's in the pantry, bottom shelf. One scoop." Did her cat know Beth was not Beth? Would anyone else guess?

"So, a teacher!" Regan said brightly. "I could do that. I could go to your school and be you." She giggled again. "Don't you remember? I played a teacher in *Long Wet American Summer.*"

Her breakout role, supposedly, but not a movie Beth had seen, though she was sure that her son had watched it several times. "That's not really funny," Beth snapped.

"Think about it!" Regan, in Beth's voice, sounded awed. "This is, like, so *Freaky Friday*. You're me, and I'm—what did you say your name was?"

"Beth Barony."

"I'm you," Regan said. "I'm Beth."

Beth fought against the feeling of sickness that surged within her at those words. "No, you're not. You're Regan Forrester. I'm Beth Barony. We can't—" She swallowed. "We have to figure out what happened here and fix it."

"Fix what?" Regan said. Beth heard the refrigerator door open again, the sound of a pop, then liquid pouring.

"What are you doing?"

"I found half a bottle of wine in your fridge, and I'm celebrating," Regan said. "My life is shit. I wanted to have a *real* life for a while, and I got my wish. How cool is that?"

4 • THE SWITCH

Beth leaned back on the bed. The pillows were very soft, the sheets of some ridiculously high thread count and probably organic cotton. Everything else in the apartment that she had seen so far was chintzy except for the bed.

How could she convince a movie star, a young, beautiful, talented—okay, somewhat talented—movie star to want her own life?

"You're not the only one," Beth said to the canopy.

Regan took a loud sip and then said, in a voice Beth now recognized as her own, "The only one what?"

"Who was thinking yesterday about how my life could be different."

What *did* you call this? There were stories of shape-shifters, stories of people changing through curses, but, aside from *The Prince and the Pauper,* people in classic novels did not switch places.

"Did you do a spell, too?" Regan sounded awed.

Beth glanced at the candles, the ashen circle. "No, nothing so—no. But I recall thinking . . . well, my girlfriends and I went to see your movie yesterday. For my birthday."

"Happy birthday," Regan said. "Was I any good?"

She wasn't, but Beth felt an urge to protect the girl's feelings. It wasn't her fault the camera made it seem like her looks were her only asset. Whatever acting talent she had, the script, or the director, hadn't given her the opportunity to demonstrate much of it.

"You were great," Beth lied. "That scene where you took down the alien king was really—vivid. All those special effects." That at least was true.

"And you saw me in my movie and wished you had a different life?"

"Something like that, I guess."

She'd been thinking she couldn't remember how she had felt at twenty-four, even though she was engaged to be married, had just finished her master's degree, and had gotten her first teaching job. She couldn't remember how it felt to be anything other than forty-two, everything already laid out for her.

She'd be teaching high school English until she retired, in a few years her kids would move out of the house and she wouldn't know what to do with herself, and her marriage had definitely become routine. She was grateful for what she had, home, family, her health, her job.

But she *had* gone to bed wondering what it was like to have what Regan Forrester had: incredible beauty, a career just beginning in an exciting industry, a toe on the threshold of huge celebrity and wealth. What would she, Beth Barony, have done if she were in Regan's shoes?

Well, here she was. In more than her shoes.

"Are you crazy?" Another loud slurp. Regan Forrester was not a delicate sipper of wine. And it was not even—Beth glanced at the phone display and added two hours—eight o'clock in the morning.

"Why would you want a different life?" Regan demanded. "You have a house, a gorgeous husband, a decent job. A dorky car, okay, but you're a real person, in the real world. I'd kill to have a house of my own. What's the problem?"

"Nothing." *Me. I am the problem.* "Trust me, I am right now feeling very keenly how incredibly fortunate I am and how great my life is. I'd like it back, thanks very much. How can we reverse this spell?"

"I don't know."

Beth was stunned. "You don't *know*?" How long was she going to be trapped here, in a movie star's life, in Los Angeles, in this admittedly quite gorgeous and sinuous body? She stretched out a leg—Regan Forrester's leg—and admired it briefly. Beth had never had legs this long and slender, not even when she was a teenager. At least she was trapped in an attractive body.

"Do you mean to tell me that you dabbled in some weird—I don't know, sorcery, and you somehow got me involved in all this, and you don't even know how to *fix* it?" She felt a hoarse screaming inside her head, like in the nightmares where she was yelling at her students for not studying for the quiz.

"Hey, your neighbor is giving me a weird look. Should I wave? Are you friends?"

"Are you back on the porch?" Beth demanded.

"Whoa! A Jacuzzi!" Regan cried.

"What are you wearing?"

A pause. "Some fake silk nightgown. Wait, is this

rayon? For real?"

Beth closed her eyes. "If you let Mrs. Henderson see me drinking on the porch in my nightgown at eight o'clock in the morning, the school board will be calling me by ten."

No, they would be calling a woman who looked like Beth Barony, but didn't act like Beth Barony. And the real Beth Barony would be—where? She hadn't asked for a different life, Beth reminded the forces of the universe. She'd just been feeling discontented. That was all.

"This is really good wine," Regan said.

Beth bit her lip. It was a sixteen-dollar bottle of cabernet sauvignon, some mass-produced label, full of preservatives to withstand shipping. She had picked up a case of it for her monthly Wine & Women book club, which met at her house the week before, since the kids were gone. Regan was not going to be of help here.

"Let's try to think this through," Beth said. "I woke up this morning as you, and you as me. Was there something specific you did that I can try to redo? Some—I don't know, some special words you had to say?"

"Yeah," Regan said, "but I had to burn them with the other stuff that he gave me. What's the big deal, anyway? Won't it just wear off in a day?"

Beth sat up. "It will wear off?"

"Well, yeah," Regan said, as if that conclusion were obvious. "What did you think?"

"Gosh, I don't know what I was thinking," Beth said. "Since this has never happened to me before."

"Why do you think they call it queen for a day?" Regan giggled.

"How much of that wine have you had?"

A pause. "All of it."

"The whole bottle?" Beth yelped.

"Duh. The *glass*. This really cute one from—what, Valleyfair? That sounds fun."

"Okay." Beth swung her long, lean, quite shapely legs over the side of the bed. She studied herself— her temporary self—in the bathroom mirror. "If it's just a day, I can do this. I'll reschedule my meeting with the dean. She won't like it, but she'll deal. The credit card will come out of the checking account automatically. You just take the day off and—I don't know. Stay at home. Watch movies. Pet the cat."

"Be you for a day," Regan said. She sounded tipsy.

"Right. And I'll be you." Beth paused. "This is what you wanted, is it?" She tried to rein in the sarcasm. That tone never worked on her daughter.

"Wow. I can do anything?"

"Just don't go skydiving or do anything else that could break one of my limbs. I don't want to wake up tomorrow morning in the hospital."

"Killjoy." Regan snorted. She heard the sound of pouring liquid again.

"No, cautious. Sensible. Please be sensible with my body," Beth begged. "It's forty-two years old, but I love it. Don't give me any tattoos. Now." She took a deep breath. "Tell me what you had planned for your day, and I'll do it."

"We're really doing this?" Her voice, Beth's voice, was high-pitched and gleeful, a tone she hadn't heard out of her own mouth in a very long time.

"I guess we are." What other choice did they have?

"I would have picked maybe a younger and hotter body, but . . ."

"Then you should have picked someone else's life to steal," Beth snapped. "That body has borne two children, natural childbirth, I'll have you know."

"Like, all natural, no drugs?"

"Not a single needle."

"That's cool. I'm totally not going to do that when it's my time. Epidural all the way. I've already decided, whenever Kevin's ready to have kids. But it's great that you're, like, this superwoman. I get to be Superbeth for a day." Another giggle, then a loud sip.

"I am not a superwoman," Beth said through gritted teeth. "I am the furthest thing from it."

"Well, I totally know how to kick butt, remember? My movie?"

"That was an alien movie," Beth said. "Everything in my life is normal." Except for this one, weird twist, but honestly, there was no precedent for supernatural body-swapping in her life, ever. Nor any hint of it in her genetics, as far as she could tell.

"Beth Barony!" Regan clapped her hands. "This is going to be *fun*!"

Beth looked at Regan Forrester's gorgeous face in the mirror and felt a lift to her heart that she hadn't felt in a long, long time. It was excitement.

She was going to spend the day as a young movie star with these lips and these cheekbones, Regan Forrester's trademark green eyes, this mane of glossy black hair, and a body as taut and toned as it was possible for a body to be. Could this really be happening to her?

"And what am I doing with your day?" she asked.

"Oh, I have no idea. Tamara will know."

"Tamara—?" Beth got cut off with Regan's shriek of joy.

"Bye, Beth! Call me later, queen for a day!"

"But you're not going anywhere, right?" Beth shouted into the phone. "Because it will be too weird if you go around in my life and—"

"Beth! Give me a little credit! I'm an *actor*. Today I am Beth. Beth Barony. I totally get your motivation. I have a backstory for you and everything."

"It's not a backstory, it's my *life,*" Beth said, but she was talking to herself. "Call ended" flashed on the phone display just as a knock sounded on the apartment door.

Beth faced her not-self in the mirror and tried to calm her racing heart. She could do this. She could last one day without screwing up her life or Regan Forrester's.

She hoped.

Queen for a day.

The woman in the mirror smiled, a sexy, impish smile, and then went, still wearing her negligee, to answer the door.

5 • THE DRIVE

Tamara, it turned out, was Regan Forrester's personal assistant. She barreled in the door at full speed, talking to Beth, talking on her phone, and jotting notes on a tablet all at the same time.

She was short and stylishly dressed in a navy suit with pinstriped trousers, with a navy hijab shot with silver thread neatly pinned around her throat. Beth's anxiety spiked. There was no way she could deceive a personal assistant into thinking she was Regan Forrester. What had made her think she could pull this off?

Tamara said, "I'll ask her," snapped shut the phone, and looked Beth up and down. "You can't wear that to the shoot."

"A shoot? What kind of shoot?"

Tamara rolled her eyes and returned her attention to her phone. "Just go put something on. It doesn't matter." When Beth didn't obey, she looked up. "Well?"

Beth blinked. "It's, um, Saturday? And six o'clock in the morning?"

"Yes, and we need to be there at seven, since the shoot starts at eight, and you know traffic in this town."

Tamara walked to the refrigerator, opened the door, and took out a gallon of orange juice. Beth didn't see much else in the appliance. She watched as Tamara took a martini glass out of a cupboard, wiped it out with a hand towel, and then took a bottle of cranberry juice from a different cupboard. She poured the juices into a glass and downed the mix in one long slug.

She saw Beth watching her. "What?"

"I could use some vodka in mine, if we have it."

Was she talking about a photo shoot? This was such a terrible idea. There was no way Beth could pull off pretending to be Regan Forrester. Regan Forrester lived her life in front of cameras. Beth Barony hated getting her picture taken.

Tamara held out her wrist and pointed at the expensive band wrapped around it. Whatever it was, it clearly also functioned as a watch.

"Right. I'll get dressed. You just—ah—hang out here."

Beth glanced around the apartment. The living area was dominated by a huge flat screen TV, the floor before it littered with video game equipment. Clothes and papers were heaped on the couch and spread across a small dining room table, which was crammed between a set of enormous speakers.

The bar that separated the kitchen was covered with food boxes, wrappers, and dirty dishes, and the kitchen itself was even more cluttered. Regan Forrester was a slob. Or her boyfriend was.

"Sorry about the mess. We... um ..."

Beth let that thought die. She had no idea what had happened in this space last night, or at any time before that. "I'll be right back."

Tamara sipped a second glass of juice and whisked her fingers across the screen of her phone.

"Don't bother with hair or make-up. They said they'd do it there."

Well, thank goodness for that. Beth snuck back into the bedroom and opened a closet. Nothing but men's clothes. She opened a different closet. Not much better. What did Regan Forrester wear on her own time? Weren't movie stars supposed to be glamorous?

Listening for sounds of movement from the outer room, Beth stepped into the closet and punched in a number. The secretary was in the office till noon on Saturdays.

"Eden Prairie High School, welcome to the home of winners" came a crisp voice.

"Evelyn, it's me." Beth smacked a hand to her forehead. She was going to have to start thinking. She'd forgotten she had a different voice.

"Excuse me?"

"Ahem. Yes, I'm calling on behalf of Beth Barony? She won't be able to meet with Dean Chavez today."

"Who's calling, please?"

Evelyn, the secretary who had seen her every school day for the last eighteen years, didn't recognize her. There was something liberating and crushing about that at the same time.

"This is—" Should she pretend to be Barony's mom? Joan? "This is . . . Barb. I'm a nurse. At the clinic."

"Barb? Are you new?" Evelyn chuckled. "I thought I knew all the nurses at the clinic."

"At a clinic out of town. In University."

Evelyn paused. "What is Beth doing at the University Hospital?"

"Long story. Just getting some tests done. Nothing infectious, we don't think. Anyway, I just wanted to tell you that Beth has to reschedule her brunch with the dean today. We can't let her be exposed to anyone until we figure out what this is."

Evelyn sighed. "Dr. Chavez won't be happy about rescheduling. Her Monday's crazy."

"It's an inconvenience, I know. I'm sorry. But there's really no way around it. I—Beth—simply can't meet her today."

She heard Evelyn tapping her pen. "What did you say your name was?"

"Sorry, I have to go—the lab results just came back. Call me—I mean Beth—with the new meeting time when you know it." She ended the call.

Across the room hung a huge poster of the TV actor from the long-ago teen soap drama that had made him famous. Kevin McDonald, that was his name. She couldn't remember that he had done any interesting work since then. The only thing she knew about him was that he was dating Regan Forrester and the relationship, by all accounts, was a rocky one.

She didn't have to have a difficult meeting with her dean today.

She didn't have to be Beth Barony for a whole day. She was free.

She grabbed a well-worn pair of jeans and a soft, cute babydoll shirt in a coy color of pink, the kind of shirt a woman like Beth Barony should never wear but a woman like Regan Forrester could and did look great in. She sashayed into the bathroom humming a tune.

The bathroom was as chaotic a mess as the rest of the place. Regan Forrester must not have a housekeeper. She thought all Hollywood people did. But Beth was pleased, if not surprised, to find that Regan Forrester's bathroom was filled top to bottom with expensive, delicious smelling, unbelievably luxurious products that Beth Barony would never know about, much less afford.

* * *

"I thought you said the shoot was at eight."

Tamara was certainly taking her time driving around Los Angeles. Not that Beth minded, since she didn't know where they were going, and she was curious.

Nothing she had seen so far looked like the Los Angeles of the TV shows and movies. Regan's neighborhood hadn't been so terrible, but once they hit the freeway, the line of cars was constant and unrelenting. The whole road was a parking lot moving at seventy miles per hour, and all around them, drivers, alone in the car, were looking at their phones instead of the road. Beyond the packed highway the sky was blurred with smog and blocked with endless buildings, the only green an occasional bristle of palm tree.

"I lied. The shoot is at nine. I told you eight because you're never actually ready on time. You want coffee?"

Beth shoved her hands underneath her legs, a nervous habit. "More than anything."

"So where did you go for breakfast?" Tamara wheeled the car onto an off-ramp.

"I haven't had breakfast yet. I woke up just before you arrived."

"Really?" Tamara lifted her brows. Perfectly shaped brows, and her eyeshadow was subtle yet glamorous. "You texted me at midnight to say that Kevin had left the club and you were going to get breakfast."

"Midnight? I texted you?"

Tamara spotted a coffee shop on the corner and swung into the turn lane, fitting her car between two approaching vehicles with inches to spare. "You don't remember? I'm so surprised."

"That was rude," Beth said, clenching her teeth. "I'm sorry."

As they idled at the red light, Tamara turned in the driver's seat to look at her. "That's the second time you've apologized to me this morning."

"It is?" Did movie stars not apologize for anything? Of course they didn't.

"I hope breakfast was worth it." Tamara joined the line of cars in the drive-thru lane at the coffee shop.

"Ah—I don't remember that, either."

If Regan hadn't gotten home until the wee hours, then when had she done that spell? More important, when could Beth expect it to wear off? "I'm thinking it wasn't all that impressive. I'm hungry. Should I get the blueberry muffin or the cranberry honey?"

Tamara lowered her phone to look at her. "Off your diet, are you?"

Whoops. "Just for today." *Sorry, Regan.*

When they finally made it to the intercom, Beth ordered both kinds of muffin, a fruit bar to save for later, and the largest size mocha with whipped cream in a reusable cup. When they reached the window Beth paused—should she offer to pay? Was she expected to? Wasn't Tamara, technically, in Regan's employ?

But Tamara pulled out a credit card, handed it to the cashier, and took the bag of starchy sweets, all while still operating her phone with her free hand. Beth decided not to say a word. She would ask Regan later if she owed Tamara any money.

"I think I'll have the blueberry. You want the cranberry?"

"Really? You know I don't eat anything processed. I thought you didn't, either."

The muffin didn't taste anything like what she made at home. Too sweet, and yet at the same time too sour as well, like it was made with all the wrong ingredients. Maybe she was tasting with Regan Forrester's tastebuds. Or maybe it was just LA, where presumably everything was different from normal.

Speaking of which, what was Regan doing with Beth's body for the day?

"Hey, if we have time, can we drive past the Hollywood sign?"

This time, with great expression, Tamara turned and lifted her sunglasses. Her light brown eyes examined Beth as if she had never looked closely at her before.

"I'm just feeling nostalgic," Beth said. "You know. For when I first moved here, all young and green with stars in my eyes." From wherever Reagan Forrester had grown up, and where was that, exactly? How was she supposed to make it through the day trying to pretend to be someone she knew nothing about?

"We're not going that way," Tamara said. "Can we do it later?"

"Yes, of course."

Beth looked out the window and ate the rest of her blueberry muffin, having the sense that she needed to fortify herself for the day. The easiest way not to screw up or draw attention to the fact that she was not actually Regan Forrester, just someone else in Regan Forrester's body, was to be as silent as possible.

But silence was not a trait anyone who knew her would attribute to Beth Barony. And what was Tamara's story, anyway? She was beautiful enough to be an actress, but here she was, working as a personal assistant, driving Beth around the city. Which she thanked God for, given the circumstances, since she would have been sunk trying to navigate Regan Forrester's life all on her own.

"So," Tamara said, not looking up from her phone. "It's time to talk about that interview."

More territory she knew nothing about. "Which interview?" Beth gulped.

"You have to ask?"

"I—uh, I don't remember much of it."

"Maybe this will help refresh your memory." Tamara touched the screen of her phone and handed it over.

The heavily made-up, perky face of a talk show host filled the small frame. Beth didn't recognize the logo in the corner but guessed it was one of those entertainment channels that catered to 24/7 celebrity news, which meant there was a lot of time spent discussing who had worn what where, who was dating or breaking up, who was cheating or fighting, and who was spending the most on their personal care, pets, or kids. Beth only went on those websites when it was very late at night, she couldn't sleep, and she had a full glass of wine.

"Next up," the host said, oozing false enthusiasm, "an interview with Regan Forrester. She's shooting into the spotlight with her recent movie *The Visitors*, which topped the list of highest-grossing box office receipts *just* this weekend, and she's been voted sexiest woman alive by three different men's magazines. Regan Forrester!" the interviewer chirped as the camera panned to his guest. "How does it feel to be on top of the world?"

"Wow," said Beth as the screen filled with the image of Regan Forrester wearing a lime green halter top and a pair of barely-there jean shorts that showed off her tanned, sleek, shapely limbs and a good portion of midriff. "You let me outside in that?"

"Yeah," Tamara said. Beth couldn't read her tone.

"I don't know!" On-screen Regan beamed in response to the host's question.

Beth was mesmerized by the girl's perfect nose, perfect lips, perfect teeth, perfect figure; it was almost unreal, how lovely Regan Forrester was. But there was something faintly off about her expression, a curl to her lip like she smelled cheese just about to turn, a look in her eye that seemed to beg for recognition and approval.

"Has fame changed me? It's definitely changed my life. I guess it's weird that I, you know, can't go anywhere—I mean, I come out of a restaurant and there's someone snapping a picture and there's a tabloid headline two days later, 'what did Regan Forrester have for lunch?' Um—a hamburger? I mean, really, who cares?"

"Girlfriend!" the interviewer squealed, waving a hand in an S shape. "You did not get all *that* going on with hamburgers! What-*ever!*"

Regan laughed, and it sounded forced, rehearsed. She sent a stray look at the camera trained on her, then leaned across the armrest of her chair. The movement pushed her breasts together and up. "I know, I eat really bad. I shouldn't. Kevin always tells me I need to improve my diet. But I just can't starve myself. I can't be one of those girls who is measuring every ounce."

"Wow," Beth said again. "Do I end up in his lap? Because it looks like I'm trying to climb in his lap."

"Glad you noticed," Tamara said.

"You have a reputation for being something of a bad girl," the reporter said, wiggling his eyebrows.

"So spill—what's the baddest thing you've done lately?"

"Bad?" The actress laughed. She tossed back her hair and combed her fingers through it, showing off her neck and, again, the cleavage. "You have no idea." She dropped her voice and said, amping up the sultry look, "I can't really talk about it. I don't want to shock people."

"Oh," Beth said. "We're bad. I have to be bad now. Is this for real?"

"That's what I want to know," Tamara said, switching lanes with an inch to spare between the cars behind and ahead of them.

"Oh, the sexiest woman thing," the girl was saying as Beth refocused on the phone. "Well, I guess it's nice, but honestly, I don't think that much about how I look."

Beth snorted. "Woman, you think about it all the time. Every single movement you make, you wonder who's watching you. Every product in your bathroom says you think about how you look every minute."

Tamara smothered a laugh but focused her attention on the vibrating, tricked-out Mustang, all its windows heavily tinted, trying to muscle into their lane. Beth clung to the phone, fascinated. This was Regan Forrester in real life?

"No, really," the actress insisted, as the interviewer also seemed incredulous. "I would so much rather be a regular person. This face—I mean, it's very lonely, actually. I don't have many friends. And no women friends. Girls just hate me."

She paused, collecting herself with another huge smile. "I get along with guys really well, but . . . I guess I don't seem to care about the typical things girls care about. Guys are just so much—you know, easier to be around. I don't have any real girlfriends. That sounds so sad, I know!"

"Oh!" Beth clapped a hand to her heart. "Poor me! I don't have any friends! I'm just so beautiful, nobody understands me, it's so hard! I don't have any girlfriends because women are just so catty and jealous and I really don't know how to relate to people unless they want to sleep with me!"

She rolled her eyes and handed Tamara the phone as the segment ended. "What are the things girls care about that Regan Forrester doesn't, I'd like to know?"

Then she saw Tamara's curious expression and remembered whose face she was wearing for the day. *You're Regan Forrester,* she reminded herself. "I was just joking. I mean, that interview was a joke. Right?"

"I was hoping you'd tell me that, but the joke is all over the Internet," Tamara said. "'Regan Forrester doesn't have any friends! Why do only guys like me? World's sexiest woman wants to know.'" She shook her head. "I have no idea where to begin with the damage control."

Beth tucked her hands under her thighs. My goodness, but Regan Forrester had beautiful legs. Tanned, toned thighs that were all muscle, slim calves, pretty knees. She even had lovely feet. Beth couldn't stop looking at them.

"But she—I must have girlfriends, right? I must."

One of Tamara's perfect eyebrows arched over the top of her sunglasses.

"Ouch," Beth said. "We're not friends?"

"You don't pay me enough for that," Tamara said. "The good news is, I think you can explain yourself today. It's for TMZ, so the questions will be pretty basic, then they want to do a shoot, and the whole thing will be online right away, so you can try to put a better spin on the woes of being so beautiful. Eve is trying to get you a spot in a weekly magazine, but you have got to get Kevin to take the leash off you for that."

"Take the leash off? What do you mean?" Who was Eve?

Tamara made a quick swerve into the parking lot of what looked like an abandoned warehouse, with a tall chain link fence around it and strange, empty smokestacks towering above the roof. "Like, he has to stop keeping you away from the paparazzi. People really do want to know what you had for lunch."

"The blueberry muffin was dry and too crumbly," Beth said. "Do better, Coffee Moose."

"That's what you get for going gluten-free," Tamara said. "I mean it, Regan. It's not just your butt. It's mine, too. And I have three kids to support."

"You have kids?" Beth almost said. "No way."

Tamara's figure was as slim as Beth's had been in high school, once upon a time. But then she remembered she was in the land of make-believe, where women had babies without developing stretch marks or saggy pooches, where people had round-the-clock nannies, and where it seemed every celebrity parent had a sideline business in designer baby wear or gourmet infant food.

"Maybe we should just call it a day," Beth said. "Go home, order in some Thai food. Talk. Bond. Get to know one another. Apparently I need friends."

She put her hands over her heaving stomach as they walked into the cavernous warehouse together. She'd spent the first forty years of her life figuring out who she was and who she wanted to be, and oh, how she wanted to go back to that person right now.

"Do something about your face," Tamara hissed.

Beth pointed to it. "You told me not to put on make-up."

Tamara circled her hand in the air. She had a perfect manicure, the tips of her fingers glittering gold. "Get rid of that lost look. That I don't know, what-am-I-doing-here, bewildered look. I never thought I'd say this, but go back to the sultry. I think I liked that better."

I've never been sultry in my life, Beth wanted to tell her, but there was no time for confessions. She had to face an interview while pretending to be Hollywood's Girl of the Moment, and Barony would fall down laughing if he ever knew his wife had paraded around as *Maxim*'s Sexiest Woman Alive for the day.

6 • MAKEUP

Inside the warehouse, the huge, open space had been turned into a photography studio, with a camera on a tripod under a set of bright lights pointing at a black fabric backdrop. One wall was lined with makeup mirrors and the other with rolling racks of clothes.

A stylist met them at the door and marched Beth directly to a sink set against the wall, pushed her into the huge reclining chair, snapped a plastic sheet around her neck, and plunged Beth's head into the basin. She started massaging her scalp with warm water and strong, expert fingers, and Beth almost groaned with pleasure.

"Can I fall asleep?" she asked, wondering when the interview was starting. It would be so unfair to ask her questions now, when she was nearly mindless with bliss.

"If you can sleep though me tweezing your brows," the stylist said.

The face Beth had seen in the mirror that morning was already perfect, but a whole team of people went to work on her. It was like when Beth had complications with Abby's birth and a flock of hospital staff swooped in.

Except this time instead of being cut and needled and lopped about, her body was tweezed, buffed, exfoliated, oiled, and dusted, propped in a chair, her head rubbed again, and something slathered through her hair. Beth tried not to choke; it smelled

45

like the chemical spray-tan she had gotten before Barony's sister's wedding.

A parade of people moved back and forth from the racks of clothes, holding different items up to her, then giving the hangers to different people whose sole function was to stand around holding things for stylists, wearing blank, uninterested stares.

When Beth went to get her hair done at her hometown salon, LaShonda chatted her ear off with news about what she, her kids, and her live-in boyfriend had been up to. There was a constant stream of information. Here, Regan Forrester might as well be a mannequin for all anyone spoke to her. Tamara took her phone, a bottled water, a stack of magazines, and disappeared.

The first second she had to herself, Beth took Regan's purple phone out of her tiny designer bag and checked messages. There was one from Beth's own number. *What's the limit on your credit card?*

Not enough to support a movie star's shopping habits, Beth thought, panicking. Barony would have a heart attack at the next credit card statement if Regan Forrester went on a shopping spree. He was already grumpy about the court case he was in the middle of; she didn't need to add high-interest debt to his list of stressors.

It's okay if you stay in today. Just text Joan that you won't be in Zumba class.

She'd been rinsed, blown out, curled, sprayed, and was getting her make-up done by a team of no less than three people, with two other people on each side of her doing her nails, when Regan's phone beeped with a response.

You could use a workout.

Beth frantically texted back. *Joan is your best friend. You love everything about her. Don't tick her off.*

"So I thought we could do this now," a young woman said, sliding into the salon chair next to Beth.

"Do what?" Beth asked warily. "I can't imagine there's a single part of my body left to groom."

The girl smirked. "You'd be surprised. After make-up there's the prep and polish, and then wardrobe wants to try a few outfits on you before Shannen does his thing. I'm Larissa Wang from *TMZ*. Okay if I record this?" She held up her phone.

"Fine," Beth said weakly, feeling overcome by the blur of names. She'd never remember any of them, but she wouldn't need to. Tomorrow this would all be a long-distant memory, like a really weird lucid dream.

"So, a few questions," Larissa said.

She looked down at a tablet in her hands and tapped at the screen. Beth admired her red plastic-framed glasses. With bows tied on her twin black ponytails, the reporter had a mischievous school-girl look going on, wearing a long-sleeved shirt with horizontal black and white stripes and a sewn-on vest, black pants, huge chunky shoes, and an enormous gold crucifix. She had clearly embraced the cliché of the trendy, sarcastic Hollywood side-kick.

"*The Visitors!*" Larissa said. "Tell me what that was like."

"Noisy," Beth said before she caught herself.

Speaking off the cuff was a bad habit developed over years of teaching, when silence in a classroom could be deadly. And, to be totally honest, she was mad at Regan Forrester right now. If anyone would guess Beth was not herself today, it would be Joan.

"They really piled on the special effects, don't you think? And it was a little long."

"Didn't see it," Larissa said without batting an eye. "So what's it like to work with Timothy Kay? What about the rumors that you two had a few tiffs on set?"

Timothy Kay. Beth tried to think. It was hard to do with five people touching her all at the same time. Was that a co-star? Director? Producer? Someone else?

"Timothy Kay," she repeated, drawing out the phase.

Larissa waggled her eyebrows. They were tweezed very, very thin and only stretched halfway over her eyes. Beth hoped they hadn't done the same to Regan's face, because Regan had beautiful, thick, dark eyebrows.

"The studio says you're all set to start shooting the sequel, they're so sure this is going to be the summer's big blockbuster. But a lot of women have said Kay, as a director, is really hard to work with."

"I don't know why they'd say that, when there are hardly any women in his movies," Beth said without thinking. "And he didn't give my character a whole lot to do in *The Visitors*, did he? The lines were basically, 'Steve, watch out!' and 'Oh no, they're coming!' and 'Do you want one cream in your coffee or two?'"

Larissa giggled and looked at her screen.

"Wow, I hope I'm getting this. All right, Regan, let's talk about your friend situation. What's up with that?"

"It's great," Beth said. "Next question?"

"Well, I thought I saw a piece on *Celebrity TMI* about how you don't really have any girlfriends. Girls who are friends, I mean."

What was it Tamara had said? Damage control. "I was a little bummed out at that moment," Beth said. "Honestly, I have tons of friends. I cherish my friendships. I have so many deep, wonderful, rewarding relationships with so many beautiful, intelligent, funny, interesting women, I can't even count them all."

She spoke straight from the heart and hoped that, if she did Regan Forrester a favor and gave her meaningful female friendships, Regan would feel obligated not to wreck Beth's.

"Gimme some names," Larissa said.

Joan. Sherice. Oh, how she missed them. How she wanted to call them right this minute and tell them about the insane thing that was happening to her. They wouldn't believe it. Her mom would have wanted to hear about every minute of this.

That ache of missing her mother came out of nowhere, tearing through Beth's stomach, undiminished by time. Mom would have mixed a pitcher of margaritas and laughed and asked question after question as Beth told her the story of the day she was having.

As Regan Forrester. Who were Regan's friends? "Tamara," Beth said. "Eve."

"Your personal assistant and your manager?" Larissa said. "That's nice."

"I spend a lot of time with them," Beth said. "Men are great, don't get me wrong," she said, thinking of Kevin the failed child actor, who had not seemed particularly friendly that morning in bed.

"But a girl has got to cherish her girlfriends. The ones who go clubbing with you when you're all young and single and who get your drunk ass home safely. The ones who will wear whatever color you put them in at your wedding. The ones you can cry to when yours kids are being maniacs. The only people in the world who will have a Lobsterita with you on every single birthday. The guys might come and go, but girlfriends last forever." She wanted Joan and Sherice so much she could cry. "Am I right?"

"I'm gay," Larissa said. "Also, I feel like my lover is my best friend, you know?"

"So's my husband," Beth said, thinking of how she and Barony used to be.

"Really?" Larissa's tiny eyebrows twitched. "You and Kevin . . .?"

"Ah. Future husband. Whenever that happens," Beth mumbled, cursing her idiocy.

Don't be Beth. Why was it so hard to remember she was in a different body? Especially when the body was so smooth and sinewy, not at all like her own.

"Finished!" said the makeup artist, and Larissa stood.

"Fun talking to you, Regan! You're a lot more real than I thought you would be. You come across as such a ditz sometimes, but today, you're awesome. Good luck with *Visitor Deux* or whatever it's going to be."

"Thanks," Beth said, without much enthusiasm. What had she said about Timothy Kay, exactly? She had the sinking feeling that she might have endangered Regan Forrester's hopes for the movie sequel. And from the looks of the girl's apartment and her personal care habits, she needed the money.

"OMG are you gorgeous!"

There before her stood Shannen, the photographer, in a chiffon skirt, fishnet stockings, chunky heels, and a tight black tank top that showed off a well-defined chest and shoulders and a pair of very hairy arms. "Are you *ready* for this?"

Beth looked into the round, all-seeing eye of his huge black camera and froze.

There was no getting around it. She was about to ruin Regan Forrester's career.

7 • THE SHOOT

There were some people, Beth knew, who were naturals before a camera. They behaved like it wasn't even there. They were photogenic. They had charisma. They could share something of themselves that translated through layers of glass and digital signals and reached the eyes and hearts of viewers.

Regan Forrester wasn't just so woefully beautiful that even hungover, on no sleep, in the frizzy early morning hours, she looked come-do-me gorgeous. Quite simply, she had no bad angles.

Regan Forrester also had that undeniable quality that poured out of her into a camera and could leave a watcher feeling mesmerized. The camera didn't just love her; it worshipped the ground she stood on.

Whatever that undefinable quality was, Beth Barony did not have it.

This was not to say that Beth didn't think she could act. Teaching was a kind of acting, all the time. She was used to being the apex of many sets of eyes. There was a mindset she could pull on, a mastery of her subject she could assume, a sense of authority granted her by being at the front of the room. She could take a breath and get into the zone, so to speak.

She'd also had something of an acting career, back in the day. She'd been the star of her sixth-grade play. The show had been taped and ran on the free public access channel so many times that by the time she entered high school, everyone in town had seen it and had an opinion. She'd joined the high school drama club and had a bit part in all the productions. In college, she'd been in an edgy, all-girl comedy improv group. They liked to try things that were definitely not mainstream. They liked to shock. It was how she'd gotten Barony's attention, tight-laced law student that he was.

But when it came to photography shoots, Beth Barony was as charismatic as a piece of taxidermy.

"Unclench your jaw, love," Shannen said for the tenth time. "You're way too tense. Quit gritting your teeth at me."

Beth took a deep breath, consciously loosened her jaw, and smiled.

"OMG," Shannen said, lowering the camera. "Are you about to eat me? Grandmother, what big teeth you have!"

"They put something on them," Beth said miserably. "It feels like Vaseline. It tastes like Vaseline, too. I'm sorry, I'm just—is this really the right outfit for me?"

She looked down at what she was wearing, or, more accurately, barely wearing. The outfit resembled Shannen's. Clunky heels laced all the way up her calf and the stand-up tulle skirt had some flounces purposely torn and falling loose. Her hose showed a few expert rips, and the tight black corset which was the only thing covering her top half had the front lacings partially undone. The trailing strings kept getting caught in her arms.

Her hair had been partly pulled back and then tousled and snarled. The mess was so sprayed it felt like a helmet and she knew she'd be hours washing it out. She very much doubted that the stylists who'd put all this stuff on her would wash it off before they sent her home.

The corset cut into her boobs and knifed her in the stomach every time she leaned in any direction. The hose itched. And the choker was actually choking her. She was starting to see spots before her eyes.

"It's Victorian Goth steampunk," Shannen said. "I totally had you pegged as a Victorian Goth steampunk kind of girl."

"Not on the inside," Beth said. She would have sighed had the corset allowed it.

"OK," Shannen said. "We're going to try this again." Two assistants stepped up to flank him with more cameras and lights. "Lean toward me. Chin down. Tilt your head to the left. No, left. No, not that much. Pout a bit. I said pout, not sneer. Shoulders back. Don't look at me. Look at Kyle. This one's Kyle," he said, waving.

"Chin again. Stop scowling. Sweetheart, loosen *up!* You're not running for public office! You're Regan Forrester and you're about to be *People* magazine's sexiest woman alive. Own it! Work it, girl!"

Be Regan, Beth said to herself. Be Regan. Don't be Beth. Shoulders back. Boobs out. Chin—what was she supposed to be doing with her chin?

"What was that, babe?"

Shannen looked at her over the camera. His assistants looked up, too.

"Did I say something?"

"Yes. It sounded like 'don't be Beth.'"

Fight to the death? Don't take meth? Beth's brain was getting too frazzled to function. She was in a daze from the constant flurry of movement, and if Tamara was right, this body had been awake until the wee hours.

"Beth is my middle name," she blurted.

Shannen frowned. "Really? Your Screen Actors Guild registration says your middle name is Joy."

"Oh. Is it?"

One of the assistants tapped her tablet and nodded.

"Oh. Well. Okay, um, I was saying 'don't be Beth' because—it's just something I do—to remind myself—not to be like that character in *Little Women*."

Shannen lowered the camera. "Excuse me?"

"*Little Women*? You've read it?"

"Um, yeah! Was assigned it, in high school, but I think I read the Spark Notes instead. Did they have Spark Notes when I was in high school?" he asked Kyle. Kyle nodded. "Which one was Beth?"

"The sister who dies," Beth said with a sigh. "She's really passive. I tell myself don't be Beth and instead be Jo. She's the one with—you know. The spunk. The ambition."

Shannen looked to his second assistant. "She likes *Little Women*. Did you see that movie?"

"How could you miss it?" said the assistant. "I cry

so hard when Beth dies."

She wiped under her heavily lined eyes. The lights gleamed on the shaved half of her head.

"I know how to fix this," Shannen said. "Go to that rack and bring me the long nightgown, the one with the lace corset. We're going to make her Beth."

Shannen's idea of a *Little Women* shoot was to make Beth a sexy tuberculosis patient. Somebody went into a prop room and brought out a bed, and a team of people busily dressed it. Beth was sent back to makeup, where much of her black eyeliner was wiped off, the red lipstick muted, several of the snarls tangled out—this took the longest—and violet eyeshadow applied to her eyes. At least she got to take off the itchy hose.

Shannen insisted she be barefoot and he fussed with the front of the nightgown until that corset, too, was partially undone. Had they been her own breasts, Beth might have swatted him, but she was getting used to complete strangers touching her body. Also, she suspected Shannen had no interest in the female form beyond the purely aesthetic.

"All right, we're doing this!" Shannen cried, bringing his assistants forward. "Be Beth!"

She did. She channeled every bit of her love for *Little Women*—a book she had read and taught at least two dozen times—and all those old improv skills came back to her. She pouted. She looked wistful. She looked tubercular. She posed in a near faint. She draped herself across the bed, then walked through sheets of billowing white fabric blown about by several fans placed around the floor.

Trying to be Regan Forrester had proved impossible, but trying to be someone like Beth March—someone she knew well, loved, and understood—was easy. It was amazing. Beth loved every minute of it.

"OMG," Shannen said, looking at a tablet screen after he'd sent Beth to change back into her normal clothes. "This was incredible. Genius! I never would have thought of it for you, Regan, but you do the sexy little sister waif look really well. New typecasting, please!"

Tamara emerged from whatever back room where she'd spent her morning, looking refreshed and happy. "Nailed it?"

"I might have done okay," Beth said, feeling euphoric. She might actually be getting the hang of this being-a-movie-star thing.

"Great," Tamara said. "I'll take you home."

In the car Beth looked at Regan's phone and every happy feeling from the past hour evaporated instantly. Below her text warning Regan not to tick off Joan floated a little blue bubble containing all caps.

OOPS.

Below it floated a laughing emoji with tears sprouting from its eyes. *LOL.*

Beth's heart immediately banged down her torso and one leg to the bottom of the flip-flops she'd pulled onto Regan Forrester's shapely feet.

Beth could cover any strangeness with Barony; he barely paid attention to her anyway. She could explain away to neighbors or acquaintances one day where she didn't seem herself. She could even patch things up at her job, if for some reason Regan ran into any of her colleagues or students.

But if the girl who didn't have girlfriends messed things up with the woman who had been the closest person in the world to Beth Barony for over twenty-five years, there was no coming back from that. No possible way.

Obviously she couldn't talk on the phone to Regan Forrester in front of Tamara. It was a long, long ride back to West Hollywood. Beth looked about for the Hollywood sign, but didn't see it.

8 · THE HIGHLIGHT REEL

"Seriously, Mall of America is right down the street," Regan said. "How can you say you never go there?"

Beth lay on the plush red velvet couch in Regan's apartment. It was long and deep but not very comfortable. Personally Beth would go for comfort over style every time, as her own home demonstrated. She was alone in the place. Tamara had left on an errand, and Kevin had sent a cryptic text.

Ur on ur own 4 latr.

On her own for what? Beth looked in the fridge for something to drink and found only bottled, deionized, vitamin-added water and an open container of some viscous green goo. She poured herself a glass of water from the tap and collapsed on the couch, wondering what Regan Forrester ate for lunch.

"What did you do to Joan?" Beth wanted to know.

"Okay, that was an accident," Regan said breezily. "I just said how we looked so good for our age, you know? And when the time came I'd pick the same person she used to get her work done. How was I to know she'd be so sensitive about it? I mean, they did a great job. It's really professional. You can hardly tell."

Beth closed her eyes and leaned her head on the armrest of the couch. It was hard and uncomfortable, like everything else about this day.

"We don't talk about her work. We act like it never happened. She did it with the settlement from her divorce case. It was emotional repair."

"Well, if your friends can't talk about it, who can? Anyway, she left, and I had to work out alone, which I hate doing. News flash, Beth, you are really out of shape! It was like trying to move my legs with eight-hundred-pound ankle weights."

Beth lifted one of Regan Forrester's long, sleek legs and admired it. Of course one didn't get these legs from sitting around eating ice cream.

"Don't count on your body getting a workout today," Beth said. "I was in and out of a corset all morning. That was workout enough. What do you want with my credit card?"

"Your wardrobe really needs an overhaul, Beth."

Beth remembered what met her when she'd opened Regan's clothes closet. "Please don't."

"I just thought I'd surprise you a little bit. When's the last time you bought something new?"

"My new navy dress with the wrap bodice," Beth said. "For my birthday."

"Yeah," said Regan. "Like, from Kohl's."

Beth sat up. "Where are you right now?"

"At your house. I came back here to shower. I hate gym showers. So gross." She could hear the girl's shudder over the phone.

Beth, of course, used the showers at the gym all the time. She decided not to mention that.

"Let's do the highlight reel," she said. "Anything good about your day so far?"

"Your neighbor is cool," Regan said. "I asked her about her swimming pool. Do you know she has, like, seventeen cats?"

"Mrs. Henderson?" Beth was astonished. "I've never been inside her house. No one has."

"She's super nice," Regan said. "Oh, somebody called from some school, saying they were the secretary. Do you want to do your meeting on Monday?"

"I'm going to have to," Beth said. "Please just text a response, please."

"Did you tell her I was in the hospital?"

Beth closed her eyes. "I told her you—I—was having tests today."

"Well, she thought I had a virus or something, or at least that's what she said after I told her it was a pregnancy scare."

"*What?*" Beth screeched.

"Yeah, that's what she said! What, are you in menopause already? Why would a pregnancy be such a shock?"

"I am not in menopause," Beth said through gritted teeth.

"Well, she loved the whole idea that you might be pregnant. She was so sad that you weren't. I wish Kevin wanted kids," Regan said with a wistful tone to her voice. "I think it would really settle him down to be a dad."

Beth had her doubts about that, but it was not her place to screw up Regan Forrester's relationship. She just had to get the girl through one day.

"Any other highlights?" she asked, hoping Regan

would say she had spent a really quiet day so far, and would spend the afternoon and evening in an equally quiet fashion. Maybe watch a movie, fire up the Jacuzzi, drink some wine. She could drink the entire bottle if she wanted. Beth would be willing to wake up with a hangover tomorrow just to keep Regan Forrester out of mischief.

Regan giggled. "Your husband's been sexting me."

Beth's stomach turned over. "Barony?"

"I don't get why you call your husband Barony. Isn't that his last name?"

"Only his mom calls him Daniel," Beth said. "What do you mean, sexting? What does that even mean?"

"Don't worry, I haven't sent nudes or anything. Nothing that would show up on the Internet. God, that's my worst nightmare. Just some flirty messages back and forth. You know."

Beth didn't know. Barony no longer flirted with her, over the phone or in person. He used to; she could remember sexy little notes, back when they were first married, tucked into her gym bag or her clarinet case when she went to rehearsals.

When had they stopped? Somewhere in the middle of law school, maybe, or when he was studying for the Minnesota bar and had been so stressed his hair started falling out. Fortunately it grew back in—Barony had thick, beautiful black hair, loads of it, even for a man his age—but the sexy little notes hadn't staged a comeback.

What is he saying to you? Beth wanted to know.

But to ask would reveal how little she communicated with her husband. If Regan wanted to know about her relationship, the text history would reveal it all. *Are you working late tonight? Can you pick up milk? Don't forget I have a meeting at eight so you have to get Abby from band practice. We're out of cat food.* So, so sexy.

When, Beth thought, had her marriage gone stale? She was married to the best guy on earth, or at least the best guy in their college graduating class. How had she let such a thing happen?

"Just don't promise anything I can't deliver," Beth said. She meant bedroom gymnastics, or whatever sex tip had been the latest feature in *Cosmo*, which she stopped reading when she was sixteen.

"Oh, Beth," Regan said in a wicked voice. "You'll deliver."

Beth sat straight up. "Don't sleep with my husband. You are not allowed to sleep with my husband."

Regan laughed. "Relax, Beth! I'm just flirting. I only thought I might buy a new outfit to, you know, make him pay attention. He's taking me out to dinner."

"He's taking *me* out to dinner," Beth corrected her. "Beth. His wife. And don't put anything on the credit card, please. I just spent half my summer school stipend at the spa."

"Don't worry about it," Regan said. "I'll figure something out. Hey, what have you been doing with *my* body all day?"

"Turning tricks on Rodeo Drive." Beth put a hand to her forehead and closed her eyes.

"Huh?"

"You had a photo shoot and an interview this morning," Beth said. "I told them you had lots of girlfriends. Apparently there's been some concern."

There was a long period of quiet on the other end of the phone. "Regan?"

"What did you wear?"

"Well, we started out with the Victorian Goth steampunk look, but I couldn't sell that very well. I will never make *America's Next Top Model*, that's for sure. So we went for a Beth March kind of aesthetic."

"A what?"

"Beth March," Beth said. "From *Little Women*. It's one of my favorite books. I think I've read it maybe thirty times."

"You read a lot of books," Regan said. She didn't tender this observation in a complimentary tone. "There are, like, bookshelves all over your house."

"I'm a high school English teacher," Beth said. "I like to read."

"I haven't read a book since high school," Regan said.

Please, God, Beth thought, switch our bodies back soon, before Regan has to interact with anyone from school. She didn't want this mix-up to cost her a job. Or a friendship.

"All right," Beth said. "Don't worry about Joan. She doesn't hold a grudge; that's one of the greatest things about her. Tomorrow I'll tell her I was hungover and grumpy and I will manage to smooth things over.

"In fact, go out and buy yourself a new dress. Go out to dinner with Barony. Have a great time. And then think about how to reverse this tomorrow, because, honest to God, Regan, I am not going to survive another photo shoot. I can't act to save my life."

"I don't think I can, either," Regan said. "To save my life? Really? Don't worry, Beth," she said, her tone soothing. "I'm going to find something that looks *great* on you. You won't even believe it. Trust me—I am really good at this."

Beth didn't believe it. As soon as Tamara left, she'd Googled Regan Forrester on her phone and read everything she could. There were several interviews and online biographies already saved as favorites. Regan Forrester kept tabs on her online persona. Beth just hoped all the girl's social media feeds or whatever they were could be dormant for a day.

Regan, she saw from the paparazzi photos, in her spare time, in her real life, liked to wear jeans with holes torn in the knees and tight-fitting tank tops. She liked gaudy jewelry and tattoos. Beth didn't need to come home to find gaudy jewelry or, please God no, a tattoo on her body.

To do her credit, Regan looked fantastic on the red carpet. She wore a designer gown well. People were probably knocking down her door to get her in their creations. But the red carpet photos all had one thing in common. Kevin was clamped onto her arm, smiling broadly into the camera like it was there for him.

In each snap he held Regan possessively, sometimes smothering her with a kiss just about the time the camera flashed. Regan tried to look comfortable, at ease, and in love, and, to her credit, she almost succeeded. She was a better actor than anyone thought. But there was something desperate in her eyes. Beth could see it.

"Okay," Beth said. "What's on my agenda for the rest of the day?"

"Didn't Tamara tell you?" Regan said. "I wouldn't know."

"No, Tamara left."

"Just walked out? Omigod!" Regan cried. "I can't live without Tamara!"

"No, I mean she dropped me—you—me off at your apartment, and then ran an errand. She said she'd be back."

"Probably lunch," Regan said. "She usually gets me lunch."

"She brings you lunch? Does that explain why there is no food in your apartment?"

"Yeah," Regan said. "I'm on this new liquid diet. Kevin set it up."

"I thought you ate hamburgers for lunch."

"As if!" Regan laughed. "Don't put that in my body, okay? I'd barf it right up."

"I would love a hamburger right now," Beth said. "A big, thick, medium rare hamburger with the works, pickle, lettuce, tomato. But I will not do that to your body, and I hope you will do no lasting damage to my credit card statement, either."

"Deal," Regan said with a laugh. "Call me later, Beth Barony. You know what? You're fun. I like your life."

I like my life, too, Beth thought as the call ended. *And oh, how I want it back.*

She went to the door to let in Tamara, bearing a paper bag full of what was revealed to be three containers of green goop in successive thicknesses.

"What am I eating?" Beth cried in dismay.

"The usual," Tamara said. "Bon appetit! And here's your dress for this afternoon."

"For what?" Beth asked, looking through the cupboards for a straw. She settled on a spoon. "I thought I would just, you know, relax around here for the rest of the day. Catch up on my favorite shows."

Tamara laughed. "As if Kevin would let you miss a premiere!"

Beth, sitting at the dining table which she'd half-cleared of clutter, paused with the spoon halfway to her mouth. "Keven said I was on my own this afternoon."

Tamara's brows disappeared into her headscarf. "What? Are you two fighting?"

"Umm. He thought I was a little weird this morning," Beth said guiltily. "Maybe that's it."

"Weirder than usual? I hadn't noticed." Beth was starting to guess when Tamara was being sarcastic, but her tone turned jolly as she hung a garment bag plastered with a name Beth didn't recognize on the jamb of the bedroom door. "You get to go somewhere without Kevin! Who will you take?"

"Excellent question," Beth said. She lifted a spoonful of green goo toward her mouth, smelled it, and put it back down. "Who do you recommend?"

"Not a guy, or Kevin will flip out. You know how he is."

Beth was beginning to suspect that she did, indeed, know what kind of guy Kevin was, and she couldn't imagine why Regan claimed to be so happy with him.

"You?" Beth gave Tamara a hopeful smile.

"What! Are you serious? You're really serious. What would I wear?"

"You could borrow something of mine, right? We're nearly the same size. I'm sorry I need a lot of hand-holding today." Beth gave an embarrassed grin. "I must be driving you nuts."

"Every day, and twice on Tuesdays." Tamara chuckled and lifted her phone to her head. "I do have a new abaya I could have somebody messenger over. But look, if I drop you off and help you walk the gauntlet, Kevin has to give you a ride home. Nasir's band is playing tonight."

"Nasir, your husband?" Beth said without thinking. Tamara arched one of those dark, polished brows.

"Nasir, the trumpet player who lives down the hall, who is also my babysitter? The kids love him but he's, like, fifteen years younger than I am."

"Those kinds of relationships work in Hollywood," Beth said innocently.

"In your Hollywood, honey. Not mine." Tamara

stepped into the hallway with her phone.

Suddenly Beth missed her own kids with a sudden violent intensity. Away at camp, they wouldn't care if their mom didn't check in for one day; they'd probably be happy for the reprieve. But she wondered what they were up to, what they were learning, who was watching out that they didn't get into poison ivy or eat too much sugar.

It was fun to play movie star for a day, but her day job, her real job, was being Drew and Abby's mom. She was good at that role. In fact she considered herself the only person who could play it.

She unzipped the garment bag and sucked in her breath as a designer gown spilled out of it. A set of shoes, dyed to match, were tucked in one side pocket, with a ruby necklace in the other. Regan was right. Amazing what a glamorous outfit could do for a girl's spirits.

She just hoped that Barony wouldn't like today's version of Beth more than he liked the Beth he'd known for the other twenty-two years.

The question of escort was trickier. She was glad Kevin wasn't taking her, with those pictures of Regan on the red carpet. She dreaded having him walk in the door at any moment. But she didn't know who else Regan might call, and Beth got the sense that she wasn't the type of person to show up at these things alone.

She picked up Regan's phone and scrolled through the contacts. Dry cleaner. Dentist. A whole bunch of names she didn't recognize. Who were the women in Regan Forrester's life?

Her thumb paused over one word that sent an old, deep pang of longing through her. Out of a reflex deeper than thought she clicked on the contact that said 'Mom' and waited for someone to pick up.

9 • THE RED CARPET

"Well, this is certainly a surprise," Regan's mom said. "Are you calling me because you don't have any friends?"

While the phone rang, Beth was swamped by the realization of what an awful, horrendously stupid thing it was to call Regan's mother for help. Who would know Regan better than her mom, be the first to suspect that something was not right with her girl? It was an atavistic impulse, Beth had to admit. She hadn't adjusted yet to not being able to call her own mother. She would never get used to that.

Before she could hang up, though, the voice came on the line, and she could tell at once she was not in any danger of being found out as a Regan Forrester imposter. Regan's mom had already started her afternoon cocktails, and her voice showed it.

Beth's heart sank. She couldn't take Regan's drunk mom to a premiere of anything.

"Just—calling to check in. Say hi," Beth said. "How are you?"

"That's what you have to say to me? After not calling me in six months? How are you?"

"Well—yes," Beth said, blinking. She couldn't recall a time when she had gone more than a day without talking to her mother, and that was in the midst of finals crunch-time. "How have you been?"

"What do you want?" Mrs. Forrester definitely sounded slurred. Beth wondered how she could get out of this conversation gracefully.

"Um, a date," Beth said. "But it sounds like you're not up to it."

"I had dental work this morning," Mom said. "Three cavities filled. I still can't feel my tongue, except to know that I keep biting it. Going to hurt like hell when the shots wear off, I'll bet."

"Sorry to bug you," Beth said. "Sounds like a bad time. I can let you go."

"Why isn't Kevin taking you? Did you finally toss him out?"

"No. Not yet."

"Well, you ought to."

Beth had the feeling she was right. "Look, I didn't know who else to call. I don't want to go alone. Do you need me to bring you something? Popsicle? Smoothie?"

"They were cavities, Ray, not my tonsils taken out." A huge sigh followed this. "At least I have something to wear."

"Do you mean it? You'll come with me? Just like that? I didn't even tell you what's going on."

"It's the premiere of the sequel for that awful movie with that one guy from the soapy high school drama Kevin used to be on."

Great. More people she was supposed to know well. This was all turning out to be a very terrible idea.

"You know what?" Beth said. "I don't feel so well. I haven't had lunch. Maybe I should just take something and lie down."

"Are you kidding? Kevin will kill you if you don't show up as his arm candy. I'm surprised he's not already there, telling you what to wear and how much lipstick you're allowed to apply." The last word came out with a definite slur.

"Is he really that controlling?" Beth asked.

"Why don't you tell me? Every time I try to tell you how bad he is for you, you cut me off for six months."

Beth wondered why Kevin had backed out of their date for the movie premiere. Had she freaked him out that much this morning? Couples were supposed to stroll the red carpet together.

Maybe he was already at the theater, supporting his friend, or enjoying some other pre-game festivities. According to the entertainment zines, he was quite a party animal, and not always with his adoring girlfriend at his side. Beth was glad to be free of him. Mrs. Forrester might prove a companion and friend in this bizarre world.

"I call truce," Beth said. "Come be my date for this premiere. We won't talk about Kevin or anything that will make us fight. And I'll wipe your face when you're drooling."

"You'll have to send someone to get me," Mrs. Forrester said. "I didn't tell you what happened to the car."

* * *

"Your mom." Tamara kept repeating this as if the words didn't make any sense to her. "You're taking your mom to the premiere."

"Is that not okay?" Beth said anxiously. If she kept making mistakes like this, raising suspicions, she might end up in a hospital ward for psychiatric evaluation with Regan Forrester's beautiful wrists in restraints. "It seems like we're talking now."

She ran her hands over the dress Tamara had brought. The clingy red fabric gleamed with spangly silver swirls. Beth Barony would never wear a dress with that plunging neckline or the thigh-high slit in the skirt.

But it fit Regan Forrester's body perfectly, and Beth felt like a million bucks in it. She thought she'd done all right with her Kohl's discounted birthday dress? The feel of a designer gown on a movie star body was the kind of high she would never experience in her own life.

Tamara scanned her from head the foot. "Good thing the morning muffin isn't peeking out somewhere. Look, I just thought you'd crossed your mom off after that last row you had over Kevin."

"Do you think he's controlling?"

"I think he's overprotective, yes," Tamara said in a neutral tone. She fastened a jeweled clip into the thick black tresses adorning Beth's head. "But you're a big girl."

She stepped back and looked into Beth's face. "You *are* acting really weird today. You never go anywhere without Kevin."

"I went to the shoot this morning with you."

"And I'm surprised he didn't check in with you a dozen times."

Beth bit her lip. The more she heard of Regan Forrester's relationship, the more worried she became about the girl. That kind of abusive, controlling behavior could look like love to someone who didn't know what else came with it.

"Maybe I need a little space."

This time both of Tamara's brows went up. "Right. If we're going to pick up your mom, we'd better get in the car. Traffic to Crenshaw is going to be hell."

* * *

The car was a limo. Of course movie stars showed up to premieres in limos. Beth couldn't remember the last time she'd been in one. A legal association Barony had belonged to rented one for some gala, but that had been ages ago. She tried to seem nonchalant as she climbed inside. Regan Forrester must ride in limos all the time.

Tamara sighed and relaxed into the plushy upholstered seat, looking happy again. "I love these."

The reminder of Barony made Beth wonder why he was taking her—or rather, Regan—out that evening. Two dates in one week was unheard of for them. What had Regan said to him? It couldn't have been his idea.

"You're miles away," Tamara said. "What is *with* you today?"

"Hmmm? Oh. I don't know." Beth stroked the red beads on her evening bag. She felt like prom on steroids. The dress, the shoes, the jewels, and the hair and makeup Tamara had touched up from the morning photo shoot—none of it was her. She didn't know what to do with herself.

Why not try to enjoy it? Regan Forrester was apparently enjoying Beth's life. Beth should try to make the most of the remaining hours of hers.

The car pulled up before the address Tamara gave. From what Beth could see of the apartment building, it didn't look any more glamorous than Regan's. A bottle-bright redhead wearing a sparkling green dress with cut outs all over the bodice shimmied to the curb, throwing a filmy shawl around her.

"A limo! I'll be damned. There's a bar in here, right?"

Regan Forrester's mom looked younger than Beth. Her skin was startling white, and she was tiny, with enormous blue eyes. Beth gaped as this glamorous woman folded herself into the backseat.

"Was I adopted?" she blurted. "Honestly, Mom, you barely look older than—" She'd almost said *my students*. Why was she having such a hard time remembering whose body she was in? Beth Barony had never looked this good in her life, not even at her wedding.

"Tamara!" Mom cooed. "Glad you're still putting up with my Ray. I thought she was supposed to be on a diet?"

"Good to see you too, Mom," Beth said. "Drugs worn off yet?"

Mrs. Forrester swept her with an assessing glance, and the hairs on the back of Beth's neck prickled. Why had she called Regan's mother, of all people?

"You know you really can't afford to put on

another pound, if you have to fit into that same costume for the sequel," Mrs. Forrester said. "Did you ask for more money this time?"

"Did I?" Beth looked at Tamara. Regan Forrester wouldn't live in a crummy apartment if she had money. She'd mentioned she was saving for a house, but Beth wondered if she was spending her money elsewhere. Perhaps on a boyfriend with expensive habits.

"You'll have to ask Eve," Tamara said smoothly. "She'll be there."

"How's Dad?" Beth asked as the limo turned onto the freeway and picked up speed.

For her, it was a natural question. But the other two women froze and exchanged a wary look.

"I couldn't care less," Regan's mother said, "and neither should you."

Beth made a mental note to find out more about Regan Forrester's father. She couldn't help but be curious about the girl's life. Beth was in her body, living in her place, being treated as the world treated Regan Forrester. It was the closest she'd come to seeing deeply inside the life of another person, and after all, wasn't this what she'd asked for, without knowing, the deepest, darkest heart of her birthday wish? She'd wanted to know what other lives looked like.

But the more she was in Regan Forrester's life, the less real it seemed.

"I don't know how to do this," Beth blurted as the limo, one of a line of limos, inched toward the movie theater. Crowds lined the sidewalk, many of them trying to peer into the shaded windows of the car. She turned to Tamara, feeling hot and cold at the same time.

"Girl honey, you've been doing this since you were six," Regan's mom said. "Didn't I teach you everything? Put your shoulders back. Don't show too much teeth. Look above, not at the camera. And for God's sake don't smile too wide, or the wrinkles will show. I think you're overdue on your Botox, hon."

"Botox?" Beth squeaked.

Regan's mom leaned forward and peered into her face. Beth flinched. Could the woman see in her eyes that a different personality, not her daughter's, was in residence?

"Cheek and lip fillers, too!" she pronounced. "Tamara is really letting you go to seed! At least the boobs and the nose job are holding up." She snorted and reached for her purse. "Best investment I ever made."

The door opened, and Mrs. Forrester held out her hand to the tuxedoed valet waiting at the curb. Beth sent a wild look at Tamara.

"Did I really have all that work done?"

Tamara blinked. "Of course you didn't. Regan Forrester is 100% natural, as American as apple pie." Her mouth twitched into a smile. "At least you're not as plastic as your mother, right?"

Beth took a deep breath and stood before the gauntlet of cameras, people, and flashing light turning to face her. She looked past them all, smiling distantly, just as Regan's mother had said. At the largest clutch of cameras, where everyone before them paused, Beth put an arm around Tamara and her mother and trusted them to hold her up.

Her smile felt like it might freeze on her face. How did Regan endure this? And how could she, Beth, possibly pull this off? Couldn't everyone see right through her?

"Really? You're going to walk right past me, luv? What've I done now?"

Beth stopped and looked up into the face of the most beautiful woman she had ever seen. Impossibly high cheekbones, a bold nose, dark chocolate brown eyes with enormous lashes, and full, smiling lips of fire-engine red. With the million-dollar face went a matching body, tall and statuesque, with a tight white sheath dress flaunting killer curves.

"Eve!" Tamara chirped. "So glad you're here. Our Regan is off her mark today."

"Gathered that when you sent out your distress call." Eve gathered Regan in a full-bodied, bosomy hug. "Darling! What's happened?"

"I think I had a rough night," Beth said in all honesty. "And I haven't felt myself all day."

Eve hugged her again. Beth leaned gratefully into her delicious-smelling warmth. "We'll deal with that later," Eve promised. "For now, just smile for the cameras, you gorgeous creature. And avoid Timothy. I think he's put out with you."

"Timothy?" Beth drew a blank.

"Oh, my! Do you not want the sequel after all? You told me you could bear it! And there is that contract we signed."

Eve began steering her down the alley of flashing cameras and shouting reporters. A few feet ahead of them, Mrs. Forrester turned her back to the photographers and looked over one shoulder in Regan Forrester's classic sultry pose. Seems she had learned that from her mother, too.

Eve. Regan's manager. Beth scrambled to put the names into their proper places. And Timothy Kay, the director of Regan's newly released movie. That name had come up earlier, hadn't it?

"What did I say about Timothy?"

"That he's not exactly advancing the feminist cause, which we all know, but he hates to hear it," Eve said through a smile that looked not at all affected. Beside her, Tamara kept her eyes straight ahead, as if willing herself to be unseen.

"I'll apologize," Beth promised. She couldn't cost Regan Forrester a film role. That was not at all part of their deal.

"Or tell him you want a bigger role, and a cut of the royalties," Eve said without changing her smile. "Your mother is certainly enjoying this, isn't she? Whatever possessed you to bring her?"

"It seemed time we made up," Beth said. Mrs. Forrester was being no help whatsoever. Far from moral support, she was hogging Regan's spotlight. Which was just fine with Beth.

Eve glanced at Tamara, then behind them with surprise. "Why, speak of the devil!"

"Is he here?" said a deep voice. Beth turned to face the black bow tie of a man advancing up the red carpet behind them. She lifted her gaze over a stubbled jaw and a set of rugged cheekbones framing sensuous lips to a pair of dark eyes glaring sternly at her.

All the breath left her body with a *whoosh*.

"We were just talking about the *Visitors* sequel," Eve said. Beth couldn't place her accent, but she loved the sound of it. "Regan can't wait."

The tall, intimidating man looked down his nose at her. It was a slightly large nose, off center in his face. Good thing he wasn't perfect, or she might start behaving like an idiot, Beth thought. She had to remember she was wearing Regan Forrester's sylph-like body and a ruby gown that showcased every line and curve. Regan Forrester was around movie-star handsome men all the time.

"I heard Regan had some complaints about her role," the gorgeous man said. "I wish you'd brought them up with me instead of *TMZ*."

"Timothy Kay." Her voice sounded breathy and faint. "I won't be forgetting *you* again."

He lifted one brow at her. "Flattered, I'm sure."

Eve gathered Beth close. "Time to move on, dear? *InStyle* wants a snap."

The other women tried to fall back as Beth reached the main bank of cameras, but she hung onto them for dear life. "Stay with me, girls. I don't know what I'd do without you," she muttered. *Don't focus on the camera. Be far away. Don't be Beth.*

Oh, how she wanted to be Beth. Right now, Beth Barony, in the place Beth Barony belonged.

"I feel like one of Charlie's Angels," Tamara said

with a giggle. "The kids aren't going to believe this."

"Regan said we're her besties, remember?" Eve leaned her head on Beth's head. "Sweet of you, luv."

"Mr. Kay! Get a shot with your breakout star?" one of the photographers called.

Beth looked around wildly. "Timothy Kay?" she squeaked. "I'm sure his date—" She bit off the words. The tall, movie-star handsome man with the unsettling eyes and off-center nose stood a few feet away, hands in his pockets, alone. He hadn't brought a date.

How could a man who looked like that not have a date? Beth's stomach fluttered foolishly as he stepped forward.

"Get my picture taken with Regan Forrester?" he said blandly. "What a treat. I'll have to get an autograph, too, or my mates will never believe it."

He was very tall. A prickle of heat moved over her skin. He wore some subtle cologne that smelled divine. Men always looked so good in tuxes. She wished she could get Barony in one more often. Barony. She must remember she was married.

Timothy Kay put his hand on the small of her waist, and every thought shot straight out of Beth's head like birds taking flight.

"Regan? What the faaa—What are you doing here?" a man's voice shouted.

A sudden fusillade of camera flashes blinded Beth, and she felt her arm yanked in a painful grip. She blinked until the stars in her eyes cleared.

"I'm coming to see the movie," she said into the furiously frowning face of Kevin McDonald.

"I thought I told you—never mind." He glared angrily at Timothy Kay, whose face was smooth and impassive. Out of the corner of her eye Beth caught the glance Tamara and Eve exchanged, but neither stepped forward to intervene as Kevin dragged Beth down the red carpet toward the entrance to the theater.

"I thought I told you not to come!" He glared about, looking to see who was watching them. Which was everyone.

"You told me I was on my own," Beth protested.

"You know damn well—" He bit the words off as a camera clicked in their direction. "What the *hell* are you doing, Regan?" he hissed under his breath. "Bringing your mother here? I told you to stay away from that crazy bitch!"

Beth tried to pull her arm away. "She's my mother!"

"She's my mother!" he mocked in falsetto. "She's a loony drunk who keeps feeding you bullshit about me, and you know it!"

He yanked Beth close and put a possessive arm around her. Beth's skin crawled with alarm. His teeth gritted, Kevin smiled at all the photographers suddenly turning their way. "Smile, damn it," he ground out between his teeth. "Don't let them think anything's wrong."

"I think you'd better let go of me," Beth said in a warning tone.

"I said smile, damn it!" he hissed, squeezing her hip.

"I said let me go, you son of a—"

"Kevin! Looking as handsome as ever, aren't you?"

Mrs. Forrester was suddenly between them, wrapping an arm around Beth's shoulder. "And still making my Ray as giddy as a princess, I see."

"Of course." Kevin bared his teeth at her as Regan's mom leaned in to give him a slurpy kiss him on both cheeks. "Great to see you, *Mom*."

He had to loosen his grip or take the full weight of Mrs. Forrester on his elbow. Regan's mom took Beth's hand and guided her down the last of the gauntlet, cameras popping like firecrackers.

Beth pasted a smile to her face and followed. No wonder all the pictures of Regan Forrester on the red carpet depicted her as if she wished she were anywhere else.

That was exactly what she wanted.

And now she was somewhere else. She was in Beth's quiet, pretty, crime-free town, consistently voted one of the best places to live in the U.S. She had Beth's credit card and was out shopping for a new dress she would wear on a date with Beth's husband, the man Beth had been in love with for twenty-two years, who treated her with care and affection.

She had Beth's body, which if not movie star quality had the advantage of being one hundred percent silicone-free. She had Beth's friends, who were not glamorous but would give up what they were doing in a second if Beth needed help.

She had Beth's house with the neatly made beds and the neatly folded laundry and the vacuumed floors and the bookshelves and the refrigerator stocked with real, edible food. She had Beth's privacy, Beth's anonymity, Beth's ability to do things without public scrutiny.

She had Beth's fuzzy bathrobe and the house slippers her grandmother had knit her and the blanket she'd inherited from her mother, along with Beth's Jacuzzi, Beth's bottles of wine, and Beth's comfortable bed without the canopy where she wanted, more than anything in the world, to be right this second.

Beth plopped down in the movie theater seat and smiled till her face felt pinched and frozen. It didn't hurt as much as Kevin McDonald's fingers digging into her arm.

She would get to go home soon. A mere matter of hours. All she had to do was not screw up Regan Forrester's life, and hope like hell that Regan Forrester wasn't screwing up hers. She'd never realized how much she loved her quiet, boring, ordinary life until it was taken away.

10 • THE GAME

"I never . . ." Beth groped through her muddled mind for something she could say that could work for—what role was she playing again?

Oh, yes, Regan Forrester, beautiful young movie star, sexpot, and pin-up for adolescent males across the globe. She was playing the part of Regan Forrester tonight. She hiccupped. "I've never kissed a girl."

"Liar!" Eve roared. In her soft accent, the word sounded more like an endearment than an accusation. "Lily Hamilton, third grade. And many more thereafter, including—never mind." She pointed a ruby-tipped finger at Beth. "Drink!"

Beth downed the shot. "How do you know *everything* about me?"

"You're not exactly a closed book, luv." Eve pushed a lock of her weave, a dark chestnut with bright red tips, behind her shoulder. "You're next, honey."

Tamara took a deep breath. "I haven't had sex in three years. Since my husband left."

"What?" Eve cried. "Liar!"

"Truth," Beth guessed. She swayed unsteadily on her seat.

Tamara nodded glumly. "Truth."

"Oh, baby girl," Eve said gently, pointing at Tamara's Italian soda. "Take a drink anyway. You need it."

"Your turn, Eve."

Beth settled her elbows on the table, pushing aside a platter. Trays empty of their appetizers covered the high tabletop among the scattered martini glasses. She'd kicked off her heels long ago and curled her toes around the strut in her bar stool.

This was unlike her, out drinking two nights in a row; she hadn't been this wild since her first year of teaching, when all the newbies went out together on Friday to celebrate surviving another week. But she was, to her great surprise, having a great time.

"I've never left in the middle of a movie screening," Eve said solemnly.

Tamara burst out laughing. "Lie. You must have to sneak out of movies all the time. Drink!"

"Truth? For real?" Beth asked. "You've never left when a movie was a complete waste of your time."

"No, girl! I paid for that ticket! You don't hop off the train halfway there, do you? You don't leave the chair with your hair half done!"

"I have," Beth said. "I do it all the time. Leave a movie if it's terrible."

"Oh really." Eve raised her thick, sharply defined brows. "Name the last movie you snuck out of."

"It was—" Beth recalled the day before, and a cold flash raked over her. She sent a guilty look at Tamara. "It was my own movie, actually. *The Visitors.*"

"You did not leave the premiere!" Eve's luscious ruby-red mouth fell open. "Kevin would have died, and then killed you."

Beth tightened the hold on her glass. "At some

point, we need to talk about Kevin," she said. "I was not impressed with his behavior today."

She'd been glad to get away from this evening's movie for several reasons, one being that it was designed to cater to the humor of twelve-year-old boys. That movie would have insulted her daughter's sensibilities; Beth couldn't bear more than half an hour of it.

She'd felt Kevin's gaze burning into the back of her—Regan's—head for the first half hour, and that, too, was enough to make her restless. Eve and Tamara hadn't complained when she whispered that she wanted to leave, and Eve picked the restaurant where they ordered course after course of tapas and a round of bracing drinks.

"But as for sneaking out of a movie," Beth said. "I went to a matinee of *The Visitors* with—a couple of people. And it was just so loud and endless I had to leave." She took a small swallow of her drink. "And I don't think I was that great in it."

Eve and Tamara exchanged a glance.

"It's a paycheck," Eve said. "And you signed a two-picture deal, so, another paycheck."

Tamara stared at the table. Beth thought of Joan and Sherice, who would tell her to her face if she'd done something terrible. They would break the news gently, hold her hand through it, and help her do better. Oh, how she missed them.

These two women might be wonderful and adorable but they depended on Regan Forrester for their salaries, or in Eve's case, part of her salary. They wouldn't steer her away from an opportunity.

"I guess it's better than underwear modeling, isn't it?" Beth said. "Only slightly less objectifying." She picked up the last delicious sea scallop and popped it into her mouth. "I hope Mom got home all right."

"I called her. She did," Tamara said. She gave Beth a questioning look. "Everything okay there?"

Beth shrugged. Mrs. Forrester had not been the ally or the soothing presence she'd hoped for. "I guess she's always like that? Noting room for improvement."

Beth's own mother had been so completely different. She demanded high standards of behavior, true, but Beth had always felt her support and unconditional love. Even now, three years after her mother's death from ovarian cancer, Beth's chest still hurt with the ache of loss.

Perhaps that was why Regan Forrester came across as insecure and unsure of herself in interviews, making provocative statements that by turns sounded callous and immature. She'd grown up having a full and unforgiving light trained on her flaws.

Then again, it was easy for a forty-two year-old woman to pass judgment on a twenty-four year-old one, even if the younger woman had seen far more of the world than Beth had.

"What do you think of my dad?" Beth asked. She wondered how big a mistake it had been, bringing him up in the car.

Again the other two exchanged a glance. Tamara pulled out her phone.

"You mean, the guy who moved back to Haiti when you were five and has never given you support of any kind, emotional or material?" Eve sipped from her glass. "If he's contacted you again, Regan, it's for his benefit, not yours."

Beth's chest hurt still, but no longer because of her mother. Regan Forrester really did not have much going for her in the way of relationships.

"I'm really glad for you two," she said suddenly. When they looked at her, she grew embarrassed, and lifted her glass to hide it. "I don't know what this girl would do without you. Honestly."

They drank, but the mood had changed from reckless merriment. Tamara hid behind her phone.

"I better go make sure the kids are in bed. I promised Nasir I'd come hear at least one set."

"Tell him we say hi," Beth said. "And Tamara, seriously—if he's of legal age?" She waggled her eyebrows. "Consider it. Three years is a loooong dry spell."

"Shut up!" Tamara laughed. "I'll see you Monday, okay?"

Beth's heart pounded. She needed Tamara to steer her through Regan Forrester's life. Tomorrow was Sunday. How would she get through a day on her own?

Then she let out her breath in relief as she remembered the spell, or whatever weird body-switching mojo she was caught up in, was only supposed to last for a day.

Regan Forrester would be back in her body on Sunday and in possession of her own life. And Beth, too, would be back where she belonged, with no one the wiser.

She leaned over and wrapped Regan's assistant in a warm, grateful hug. "You saved me today. Thank you."

Tamara reacted as if she'd never been hugged before. She patted Beth awkwardly on one shoulder, left bare by the plunging back of the dress. "Um. You're welcome. Monday it is!"

Beth settled back with her drink and looked around them. The bar was filling with good-looking, well-dressed people all laughing and talking in small groups. Pounding music played at a low volume, and muted neon lights glowed in different colors from hidden pockets along the walls. A server with short, spiked red hair and a pierced nose, a tuxedo jacket, and a lanyard with the pronouns "they/them" swept by their table to collect empty dishes.

Beth smiled at them. "Thanks."

"Uh huh," they said with a flicker of a glance. "Anything else?"

"I thought I'd be recognized everywhere I went in public," Beth said to Eve. "I thought I had paparazzi chasing me all the time."

"They're a little more subtle here." Eve nodded toward a couple who stood a few tables away, posing while a friend held up a cell phone pointed in their direction.

"Totally gonna photobomb this," Beth said.

She leaned forward, picked up her drink, and stared at the phone with an exaggerated, open-mouthed grin as it flashed. The couple immediately grabbed the phone, looked at the picture, and laughed.

"We'll tag you," the guy called, giving Beth a thumbs up.

"You'd better." She waved her glass in response.

Regan Forrester, as a celebrity, must have at least one or two social media channels that she updated regularly in order to keep her fans happy. Most likely they involved pictures of her in revealing clothing making a duckface or showing cleavage. Beth wasn't about to do either of those things.

How glad she would be tomorrow to go back to her anonymous life, where she didn't need to be conscious of cameras, and where she intentionally kept no social media profile because she didn't want her students to know about her life outside of school. Beth Barony had no fans and no followers and preferred it that way. She had kids whom she missed acutely. She'd email them first thing in the morning. Beth Barony had a whole contact list full of friends, and she was going to call every one of them tomorrow.

Beth Barony had a husband she'd been faithful to for twenty years. And he had been faithful to her.

A cold clutch of fear traveled up her legs. Regan Forrester had better not sleep with her husband.

She grabbed Regan's phone and sent a text. *How's your DATE?*

Eve set down her drink and gave Beth a curious look. "You know, I like you like this."

"Like me how?" Beth watched the phone, waiting for a reply. Seconds passed.

Eve tilted her head to this side. "Like this. Relaxed."

Beth laughed and put the phone down. "Relaxed?"

She'd been as stiff as new leather all day. Relaxed was the furthest thing from what she was feeling. Who could be relaxed in another person's body, in a suddenly strange and different life?

"No, I mean—genuine." Eve's brow furrowed. "I'm not sure how to explain it. It just feels like— you're finally not trying to be someone else."

Beth had to laugh at the bitter irony of this. She *was* someone else. She was Beth Barony wearing Regan Forrester's skin. While Regan Forrester was, at this very moment, wearing Beth Barony's skin, and quite possibly Beth Barony's husband. Funny how easy it was to accept something so truly outrageous. Any second now, she would wake up in her own bed, with Barony beside her. Making love to *her*, not someone else.

"You mean the persona? It's exhausting to have to be on display all the time. To be that sexy, all the time." Beth gestured toward her companion. "I mean, you woke up this gorgeous, but the rest of us—it's a lot of work, isn't it?"

Eve narrowed her eyes thoughtfully. "It's not like you to be so free with the compliments. But yes, if you want the payoff, you have to do the work."

Beth snorted. "Do the work. That's what I tell my—" She bit off the rest of that before she sounded foolish. Eve was already looking at her with close consideration.

"Tell who?"

My kids, Beth had been about to say. *My students.* But Regan Forrester didn't have kids or students. She didn't, from what Beth could tell, have anybody, not really. She had a personal assistant who steered her through the responsibilities of her role and a boyfriend who controlled every aspect of her existence. She was alone, and vulnerable, and lost.

No wonder she had wanted to escape.

And now Beth couldn't wait to bring her back.

"That's what I tell myself," Beth said. "Hard work." She glanced at the blank display of the phone, then put it aside. What were they *doing*? "Do you know how I get ahold of Benny?"

Eve stiffened, her eyes growing wide. "Bene?" she echoed. "Stay away from that business," she said. "Far, far away. You hear me, girl?"

"I would, except—" Beth wasn't sure how far she wanted to go with this. "His name is Bene?" Kevin had called him Benny. How like him to mispronounce a non-English word. "That's Italian. It means good," she said before she caught herself. Eve wasn't one of her students. And Bene couldn't be a bad guy, with a name like that. "He's kind of brought the business to me."

Eve put her elbows on the table, chin in her hands. "You gonna tell me about it?"

"I can't," Beth said guiltily.

It would wear off in the night, wouldn't it? Whatever Regan had done, it would simply go away. It had to.

"Fine. I have to go." Eve picked up her evening

bag. "Do you have a way to get home?"

"Call a cab, I suppose," Beth said. At Eve's look, she panicked. "LA still has taxis, right? Uber? Something?"

But Eve was staring over her shoulder at a new group that had entered. They went to the set of couches near the front window. "He's here," she said in a significant voice.

Beth blanched. "Bene?"

She wasn't sure she was ready to confront him. She wanted out of this situation, true, but this Bene, whoever he was, was dealing in some dangerous forces. Against-the-laws-of-physics kind of forces. Beth didn't want to get any closer to that than she had to. Her stomach flipped over.

"Timothy Kay."

Eve tilted her head toward the tall man who stood talking to a group of young women. They fluttered and laughed and preened. All of them were gorgeous, perfectly formed, and very young.

Beth's stomach flipped back. Then, when he looked up and spotted her staring at him, it danced around a little more. She abruptly turned around.

"He's coming over here," Eve said out of the side of her mouth.

"So?" Beth downed the last of her drink.

But she couldn't pretend to be unmoved when the tall form appeared at her elbow in a dark jacket and a scent that whispered *man*. Beth had always been attracted to dark-haired men, and this one reminded her of Barony during his law school years. He was taller, leaner—Barony had broad shoulders and a barrel chest—and stubble covered his jaw. He needed a haircut. His cologne was amazing. It made something warm curl up in her belly and nestle in.

She hadn't felt attraction to another man since she'd married. It was a betrayal of her husband.

Beth tried to calm her panicked thoughts. She was in Regan Forrester's body. Regan Forrester felt attracted to Timothy Kay. Her director. Her boss. A man at least ten years older than she was, but who possessed a careless, easy charm. And a dark, smoldering gaze currently pointed in Beth's direction, taking in the barely-there neckline of her gown and the waves of black hair floating around her shoulders.

"Are you all right?" he asked her.

"Of course I am." Beth reached for her glass and found it empty. "Why wouldn't I be?"

The dark eyes stayed on her, considering, careful. "Your boyfriend seemed upset with you at the premiere." He glanced at the empty stool. "I assume he's here?"

"That was Tamara's seat, but she left." Eve slid to her feet. "I'm on my way as well. Did you enjoy the screening?"

"Very much." His lips twisted in a half-smile. He had a very interesting, well-shaped mouth. "My movie won't be the worst of the season, with that turd about to be released."

Against her will Beth laughed. "That's true."

"It will give the critics something to do." His eyes slid over her shoulders, lingering on her collar-bones. Beth shivered as if his hand had caressed her, not just his eyes.

"If you're on your own, you should join me. We can talk."

He strolled back to the set of suede couches, where a group of women converged on him again. Beth carefully set down her glass.

"I should go, too. I imagine Kevin would have fits."

"Oh, yes," Eve said. "We mustn't upset Kevin." She threw a scarf around her neck. "You know, many women would not mind talking to Mr. Timothy Kay. As long as he was very, very close. And whispered in their ear. While in their bed. Without clothing."

Beth tried to ignore the shiver that ran through her. She felt the same. No—Regan Forrester felt the same. Danger lay in that direction.

"Maybe you should take him home, then."

"I have a client under contract to him," Eve said shortly. "Conflict of interest." She tossed back the end of her scarf, gathered her bag, and then her face softened. She leaned down to kiss Beth on the cheek. "Be careful, luv. Very careful."

"I'm heading home." Beth was glad Eve picked up the tab. Regan was no doubt paying in some way for all of this. Hopefully a set of appetizers and a few drinks at a classy Hollywood bar balanced out whatever Regan had spent sprucing up Beth Barony today.

What *was* Regan doing? She imagined the worst. Regan and Barony, curled in bed sipping wine while the electric fireplace threw patterns of orange flame and sexy, nubile Regan Forrester did things to Barony that Beth had never imagined or dreamed.

She was in Beth's body, true. Which meant Barony wouldn't even know he was cheating.

What if he liked Regan Forrester better than he liked Beth? What if he fell in love with her? He'd been distant from Beth for a while. Years, to be honest. Wrapped up in his work, while she went about her own routine. They were co-parents and partners, a well-oiled machine, keeping the house running and the kids happy. But they hadn't behaved like lovers for a long, long time.

What if he was discovering all that again with Regan Forrester? What if everyone liked Regan better than her? What if no one in her life wanted Beth Barony back?

Against her will and better judgment, Beth's feet carried her to the couches where Timothy Kay stood talking with his group. She didn't want to be left on her own just yet. And she certainly didn't want to be back at that shabby apartment with Kevin.

Timothy Kay smiled at her and pointed to one of the couches. The other girls melted out of her vision. She sat in a corner of the couch, and Timothy Kay sat beside her, his hip butted against her hip, his long thigh pressed against the length of her thigh.

He felt hot and firm and he smelled divine, and when he laid his arm across the back of the couch, his thumb brushed her bare shoulder. Beth sucked in her breath. She tried very hard not to snuggle against him. How long had it been since a man showed any interest in her?

She didn't want to think about that.

"What did you want to talk about?" she asked.

"Your comments in your interview."

He looked into her eyes, his face quite close, his attention entirely focused on her. Beth kept her hands in her lap. Would he know he wasn't speaking to Regan Forrester? It felt like he might be the first person all day who would notice.

"The one about how girls don't like me and I don't have any friends?"

"I assume you were out tonight to disprove that. I mean the remarks you made this morning about how I was hard to work with."

Beth flinched. "Did I say that?"

"The reporter called me right away to ask if I had any comment." He looked amused, not angry, but there was something watchful and potent in his eyes. "You said, if I remember correctly, all I had you do was flash cleavage and ask how people wanted their coffee." The dark eyes gleamed with mischief. "And yet I don't recall shooting a single scene that involved coffee."

"I also didn't show any cleavage. Or not much," Beth said. The costume had completely covered her torso, but since it was skin-tight, it showed every curve nevertheless. Cleavage was beside the point. "I assume you know what I meant."

"Maybe," he said in a low voice, not taking his eyes off her face, "you should tell me what you meant. I assume that, if you have a problem with the movie, you would come to me about it."

"Of course." Beth fidgeted with her bag. "I would. I am. I mean, that's what I'm doing right now."

"Oh." One dark eyebrow arched. "Well, then. What do you think of the script for the sequel?"

Beth looked at her hands. "I—uh—haven't read it yet."

The second dark brow joined the first. "Really? Yet I sent it to your manager two weeks ago. Perhaps you've been too busy being out and about."

"Promoting the movie," Beth shot back. She wasn't going to let this arrogant, dark, sexy man intimidate her.

"Which you said was noisy." His voice was a husky rumble. "Do you have any ideas for the sequel?"

"As a matter of fact, I do." She curled her hands around her bag. It was hard to feel very sassy when she was crammed into a tiny space, his entire body unfolded beside hers, that delicious cologne wafting under her nostrils. The pulse of the music overhead had somehow found its way into her veins. A deep, prickly heat coiled in her belly.

"I think you should give me more to do." Surely Regan Forrester would ask for what she wanted. What did Regan want? For her career? For her life?

"These movies can be so much better than adolescent fare," Beth said. She was cribbing Beth Barony here, but something about the intensity of Timothy's stare made her daring. "It's an epic story, and it doesn't need a ton of CGI to get the point across. I think you should give my character a backstory, and an arc, and maybe a whole cohort of powerful superwomen that she works with and can call up to fight the next invasion."

She was rolling now. "You need to get some women in the audience. We love movies too, you know. But don't make the villain another bitter woman foiled in her ambition. We're tired of being told that ambitious women are evil. Choose a handsome, charismatic older man, someone very sexy. And give Steve more of a moral conflict. Make us more of a team instead of me as the romantic squeeze. There can be more character conflict and fewer explosions and it can still be good."

He regarded her in silence, his eyes moving over every inch of her face. Beth was glad that Regan Forrester had such a perfect face. A man like this wouldn't look twice at Beth Barony. He wouldn't even see a Beth Barony as a woman. But he was looking very, very closely at Regan Forrester as if he were noticing her for the first time.

"Those are all very interesting ideas." He sounded surprised. "Most of them won't make it past the producers. Believe me, I tried with the last one. But I can try again."

"Glad to hear it." Beth clutched her bag and gathered herself to rise. "Thanks for your time."

His arm brushed her shoulder. The hairs on the back of Beth's neck rose straight up.

"I'll take you home," he said.

She knew what he meant, but the way it sounded made her shiver. How long since a man had wanted to take her home? Barony took for granted that she would be there. She felt young and reckless in this fresh, hard, sculpted body. She'd forgotten what it felt like to have male attention, or indeed any attention.

"That's very chivalrous of you," Beth said. "I'm sure I can find my way." Actually, she had no idea how to get to her apartment from here, but she had made note of the address when Tamara drove them home earlier that day. It seemed information she should be aware of.

"And I'm sure your friends here will miss you," she added, nodding at the bouquet of pretty young things perched on an opposite couch. "And your wife," she went on, wondering where she found the nerve. "And your kids."

"My wife and kids don't care," he said, rising as she stood, "since they lie far in the future, if ever. And my friends here couldn't care less." He put a hand under her elbow, guiding her to her feet. "I have a driver waiting outside."

The inside of the car was close and dark and quiet, the tinted windows keeping out the glare of the passing city lights. Beth ran a hand over the plush upholstery. She'd miss one thing about Regan Forrester's life: the gorgeous fabrics.

Timothy Kay didn't try to make a move. She was grateful for that, really. He sat in the opposite corner, his face in shadows, and they spoke of films, his, hers, future projects they'd like to do. He was surprisingly easy to talk to. It was almost like chatting with Barony, save for the constant prickle of sexual awareness.

The car pulled up to the curb before her building,

and she saw the look pass over Timothy Kay's face. He, too, was surprised she lived in such a crummy place.

"I'm saving up for a house, so I'm hoping to get a really good offer on *Visitors 3*," she joked as the driver walked around and opened the car door. That was another thing she'd miss about Regan Forrester's life: people opening doors for her. Beth Barony had to open doors for herself.

"You'll be okay?" His voice was a low purr in the darkness. Beth caught one last whiff of him and her toes curled in her designer shoes.

"Yes." The dark apartment windows meant the place was empty, or her roommate—Regan's boyfriend—was asleep. She'd be glad not to have to deal with him tonight. And so, so glad to wake up in her own bed tomorrow morning. Glad for all of this to be a distant dream.

"I've enjoyed this. We should do it again."

"That would be nice," Beth said wistfully. She, of course, wouldn't be around for it. But she hoped Regan would dump Kevin and move on to a nice man like Timothy Kay.

Okay, he wasn't exactly nice. He was potent and dangerous and mysterious and very, very attractive. But he was also a grown-up, a man who knew what he wanted and knew how to get it. That was attractive, too.

She felt the crazy impulse to lean over and kiss him on the cheek. She knew she shouldn't. He was Regan Forrester's boss. She couldn't give him any ideas. She was Beth Barony, soon to be back in her own skin, and she'd never kiss another man aside from her husband.

But as she stared at him, he lifted her hand and kissed the back of it. His stubble grazed her skin and a warm gush splashed into her belly. She heard her indrawn breath.

"Be nice to Regan, okay?" she said, her voice a whisper. Why was she trying to be Regan Forrester's mom? Because she didn't have one, not really?

"This is her life on the line. This movie could make or break her." She hesitated. "If it's a break, I'd rather it be a good one."

"I can be very, very nice to Regan Forrester," he said. His voice scraped over her skin like a velvet brush.

Beth pulled herself out of the door. "Good night," she said firmly.

The apartment was dark and empty. Beth heaved a sigh of relief. She took a hot shower, brushed out all the hair product, and washed everything off her face. Then she pulled on a worn-out old T-shirt and a pair of gym shorts and crawled into bed.

This day was too much to think about right now. She'd deal with it all in the morning, when she was back in her own life. Right now she wanted to think only of her life, Beth's life, to make sure she got back there. Beth's home. Beth's family. Beth's familiar skin. It would feel so, so good to be home.

She waited a long time, in the dark, before all thought drifted away.

11 • THE ARGUMENT

The sound of furious pounding swooped into her dark place and pulled Beth out of sleep. For a moment she thought it was construction starting up down the street. They were building a new house at the end of their block. But this wasn't a jackhammer. It was someone pounding on a door with his fists.

"Open up! What the hell, Regan? Let me in!"

Regan? Who was Regan? Beth blearily groped for the edge of the covers to throw off the heavy weight holding her down. A friend of the kids? But weren't the kids—?

Her body didn't want to obey her mental commands as she wrenched herself upright. Her limbs felt stiff, her head full of stuffing. What was she thinking, to go out drinking two nights in a row? At her age! She wasn't in college anymore.

She stumbled out of the bedroom and crossed the next room. A feeling of wrongness registered, but the pounding was insistent, and her head hurt. She pulled back the chain, struggled with the deadbolt, and opened the door to the angry face of a guy who used to act in a teen show she'd watched at least twenty years ago.

"Why in God's name are you pounding on my door!" Beth shouted.

"What the *hell*!" he shouted back. "You locked me out? You bitch!"

He tried to shoulder through the door, and out of reflex Beth pushed it shut on him. A moment the later the door slammed inward, clipping her on the shoulder, and she stumbled backward with a yelp. The man stormed in, fists clenched, face twisted with rage.

"I can't *believe* you! That you would—me, of all people—" He shoved his face close to hers. "You filthy, stupid, worthless little whore—"

It was the actor. Kevin McDonald. Regan Forrester's boyfriend. She was in Regan Forrester's apartment, Regan Forrester's body, Regan Forrester's life. Still. Nothing had changed.

Beth opened her mouth and screamed as loudly as she could.

The impact of his hand on the side of her face silenced her, as he'd meant it to. Her ears rang, and tiny lights danced across her vision. She'd always thought that was just an expression, seeing stars. Out of instinct Beth went into a crouch and scrambled backward until she ran into the solid shape of the couch. She jumped on it and then over the back.

She landed in a pile of something that slid beneath her feet. Video games. Regan Forrester's apartment was still a filthy mess, and Beth was still trapped in it, but the first thing she had to do was get away from him.

She laid a hand over her stinging cheek. "You hit me!"

"I should do worse!" he shouted. "After the way you behaved yesterday? Sneaking out of the premiere—going off to get drunk with those little whores you call friends—and Timothy Kay! What the hell was that! Did you invite him in? Did you sleep with him?"

Beth eyed the door. He could cut off her escape if she lunged for it. She could run into the bedroom, or the bathroom, but he might be able to break down the door. He was big, and he was furious. She prayed he didn't have a gun. She would likely survive a beating. But if a gun were available, the chances of a domestic violence incident turning into domestic homicide increased exponentially. She knew that, thanks to Joan.

"I didn't sleep with Timothy Kay."

Beth tried to keep her voice even and calm. If she kept shouting or screaming, she was sure to anger him further. Cold fear gripped her, icing her back, clamping around her ribs. "I didn't get drunk with the girls." That was a lie. Her head said she had the mother of all hangovers, but that was also pure terror pounding through her temples. "I left the movie because I didn't like it. None of that had anything to do with you."

"You made me look like an idiot," he snarled. "Tramping around with that asshole! He made a pass, didn't he? I knew he was going to! I told you not to take that role!"

"He didn't touch me."

Another lie. He'd kissed her hand, and she'd shivered all over, feeling that kiss in places that had forgotten the potency of unfulfilled desire. Beth held very still, as though she were trapped in a cage with a wild animal. McDonald paced back and forth before the couch as if he were one, gnashing his teeth.

"He wants to. The way he uses you in his movies, drapes you over everything, makes you wear that skin-tight shit—and you love it. You love showing it off." His burning glare raked over every inch of Regan Forrester's perfect body. *Her* body, right now, that would feel every bruise if he got his hands on her. "You eat it up like a stupid, filthy little—"

"Stop it!" Beth shouted. So much for keeping calm. "I did not sleep with him, and that's the end of it. Either you believe me or you don't." She lifted her chin.

"Either I—!" His astonishment was overtaken by a deeper rage. Fear clutched Beth's heart. She'd never, ever felt in danger for her life before.

She stood frozen to the spot, too scared to run, too scared to think. *Please don't let him kill me.* She didn't want to die here. What would happen to Regan Forrester if Beth got her body killed by her insane boyfriend? What would happen to Beth?

"You don't talk to me like that, you piece of shit! You show a little respect!"

He crouched as if he meant to vault over the couch at her, his hands curled into claws.

Beth sucked in air for another scream. "Touch me and I'll call the police."

It was a bluff. The phone was in the bedroom, on the nightstand next to her bed. There was no landline anywhere that she could see. Her one chance of escape was to get out of the apartment, run down the hall pounding on doors.

Who would help her? Who was awake?

"You wouldn't dare."

He froze, glaring at her. "It would end your career. I'll tell them about you."

"It would end yours. That I promise you." Beth didn't know what he did for income. He didn't have a job that she could see. In all the online biographies she'd read, the one thing he was known for was being Regan Forrester's boyfriend. Panic pressed at her lungs, pushing out all the air. She had to get away from him.

"I'll kill you if you don't start listening to me," he whispered. "I will."

"I'll tell the police you said that." Beth fought to keep her voice level, look him in the eye, not show fear. Men like him fed on fear. "Unless you get out of here, right now, leave and never come back. Don't talk to me, don't call me, don't touch me, don't look at me. Take your things," she added, looking around at the squalid mess of the apartment, "and go."

"You can't kick me out!" he roared. "You *bitch*! I will—" He gathered himself to launch, and Beth readied herself to sprint for the door.

There was someone in it. A huge man, then a smaller woman, both in dark blue uniforms with a badge on their chests and equipment belts wrapped around their waists. Relief hit, so strong it nearly made Beth fall over. She wasn't alone with him. The police were here.

"The neighbors called about a disturbance."

The man's voice was a deep bass rumble. He looked back and forth between Beth and Kevin. "Everything all right here?"

Not an eyelid flickered on his face or that of his companion. They'd seen this, Beth thought, thousands of times before. Thank God for the neighbor who had called the police, rather than bolting her door and deciding a domestic dispute was none of her business.

But, oh God, the police were here. This would be in the papers. Everyone would know the truth about Regan Forrester's life. McDonald was right; her career *would* be over.

Kevin threw his shoulders back, forced his fists to unclench. Beth saw the muscle working in his jaw. "Everything's fine. You must have the wrong address. There's no problem here, officers."

Beth drew in a deep breath. This wasn't her life; it was Regan Forrester's. She couldn't mess up Regan Forrester's life. But she, Beth, did not want to die in Regan Forrester's body. She had to buy them both time. She needed to survive long enough to figure out how to get her own body back and make sure it was safe for Regan to return.

"He threatened me," she said. Her voice wobbled. "I've asked him to leave."

Kevin glared at her. "She's lying. We were just talking."

Beth swallowed a sob. "I'm asking you now. Please leave." A different fear hooked its talons into her. "It's my apartment, isn't it?" Oh God, if she had to leave the apartment, where would she go? She didn't know anyone in this town. Who would take her in? What had she done?

Kevin cocked his chin at the police. "I live here. She's making this up. She does this all the time."

The male officer raised a black eyebrow. His head was shaved. His head nearly touched the doorframe. He was not someone Beth would want to mess with.

"Ma'am? Do you still want him to leave?"

The sobs were perilously close to the surface. Beth lifted her chin. "Yes, please, officers."

The man took out a small pad of paper and clicked a pen. "Let's step out here a moment, Mr. McDonald, and you can tell me exactly what happened."

"This is my place!" Kevin shouted. "All my shit's here!"

"A moment," the officer said in a hard voice, gesturing toward the hallway, "of your time."

Kevin hardened, clenching his fists again. The female officer stepped close to Beth.

"Ma'am, if you feel there have been threats of violence against you, you can file an emergency protective order," she said in a brisk, firm voice. She was half a foot shorter than Beth, her long hair wrapped in a lush bun at the back of her head, and she was probably fifteen years younger, too. Beth wanted to sag in her arms and weep.

"There's no evidence! I didn't make any threat! You can't take me—"

Kevin crouched and leapt. The tall officer in the doorway casually extended one huge muscled arm.

Before Beth knew quite what had happened, Kevin McDonald was face down on the floor with the female officer straddling his back, slapping handcuffs on his wrists. "You have the right to remain silent," she began, reciting the words Beth had only ever heard on the detective shows Barony loved to watch. With calm strength, she helped McDonald to his feet and handed him over to her partner.

Kevin pierced Beth with eyes like knives. "Don't you do this," he spat. "Don't you dare do this. You hear me? You know what I'll do!"

"Anything you say can and will be used against you in a court of law," Beth said shakily.

"That's my line, ma'am." The tall officer took Kevin's arm and led him into the hallway. "Anything you say . . ."

The female officer, all business, took out her notebook as well. "Miss Forrester, I'm Officer Vega. Can you tell me what happened here?"

The front of her notebook was pink and decorated with glittery stars. It looked like something Abby might do to her school books. Beth's knees gave way. She groped her way around the couch and sat down. She might faint, or vomit, or both. She missed her daughter so much it felt like a blade slicing through her. Would she ever see her kids again?

"You know who I am?" Or rather, was pretending to be. This felt more surreal than anything that had happened yesterday. How could she protect Regan? How could she protect herself?

The officer's eyes twinkled. "Loved you in *Long Wet American Summer*."

Beth closed her eyes. "Have you—is this—" She drew in a steadying breath. "Is this the first time I've given a report?"

"I'd have to look at our files for that. If you want to press charges for anything that happened here, there are some steps to go through."

The officer sat beside her. Her navy uniform, neatly pressed, reminded Beth of Barony's favorite suit, the one he wore to all their weddings, funerals, and holiday parties. How she missed her husband. What she would give to wake up in their queen-sized bed right now and find him snoring beside her, one hairy leg sticking out from beneath the covers he'd hogged to his side.

Not once, in their life together, had Barony ever raised his voice at her. It would never occur to him to threaten her, or anybody. His mind was methodical, logical, prone to solving problems. She might have resented, now and again, that he lacked spontaneity, impulsiveness, passion. But she'd never seen him in the grip of rage, either. What she would give for his calm, sturdy presence right now.

"Kevin just made threats. Mostly."

Beth touched the side of her face, which stung. How long had he been like this this? How long had Regan stayed with him out of fear or coercion?

Or had Beth pushed him over the edge? She had promised not to ruin Regan's life.

He'd said he could expose something about her. What?

"I happen to know he's under court-mandated anger management classes after a different incident," the officer said. "An EPO, an emergency protective order, would last five days and give you enough time to file a restraining order, if you felt you needed one. The court can explain the different types."

Her dark brown eyes were soft and full of compassion. She, too, had never been with a partner who mistreated her, Beth guessed. But she saw this all the time. It happened all the time, and it didn't matter how young or gorgeous or famous or rich a woman was. Regan Forrester, sexiest woman alive according to several magazines, had been living in painful relationship for who knew how long.

"I don't know about charges or a restraining order," Beth said. "I'll have to decide." Regan would have to decide. Beth would be free and clear and out of here soon, back in her safe, calm, violence-free life. She didn't know how she was going to get back there, exactly, but she would. She had to. "Let's start with the EPO."

When the officer left, Beth went to the refrigerator. The only thing in it was yesterday's green goop and half a carton of orange juice. She stood with the door open and drank straight out of the carton. She yelled at her kids for doing that, but she didn't know which cabinet Regan kept her drinking glasses in.

She wasn't sure the orange juice would stay down—the hangover was getting worse, now that the adrenalin was leaving her system. Some of it dribbled down her neck into the collar of her beat-up shirt and onto Regan Forrester's cleavage.

She was wearing this perfect body, and she was too scared and tired and sick and angry to enjoy it. What a joke. Beth went to the bedroom and found the phone.

Regan answered on the first ring. "Hi, Regan!" Her voice sounded bright and bubbly.

"You're Regan. I'm Beth," Beth snapped. "What's going on?"

"Barony's taking me to Mall of America! I'm so excited. I can't believe I've never been." Her voice moved away for a moment. "Babe, why don't we go to Mall of America all the time?"

"Because you hate shopping," came Barony's low rumble.

Beth clutched the phone, her throat catching. Barony, beloved Barony. So steady. So solid. So safe. He sounded in a good mood. It was nice to hear him in a good mood; he'd been worried and pensive lately.

"Well, today I love shopping!" Regan chirped. "We're going to have a great time."

Beth wanted to scream. She was lost and stuck in a crummy apartment in Los Angeles, alone and friendless, with a raw face and a throbbing head and a stranger who had just threatened to kill her, while Regan Forrester had Beth's body and Beth's husband in Beth's car headed to the Mall of America, a place Beth actually hated, but which right now sounded like the most wonderful place in the world.

"Did you sleep with my husband?" Beth sobbed,

clenching the phone till her fingers hurt.

"Um." A long pause. "We had a great night. That was a great night. Wasn't it, babe?"

"You don't get to call him babe!" Beth shrieked. "You slept with my husband! I can't believe this! You slept with—"

"Hey!" Regan was giving her the cool-it-now mom voice. She recognized that tone. "I went out to dinner, with *my husband*, and we had a great time. He's finally wrapped up that case—what were you working on, babe? That big case? It's all done now. So we celebrated."

"The Cates case is settled?" Beth's head pounded. "Barony won?"

"I'll tell you all about it later," Beth's voice chirped back at her. There was a giggle, another rumble from Barony, and then, "Okay, maybe not *all* of it. Barony says there have to be some secrets." She giggled again.

"You slept with my husband. That *has* to be against the rules," Beth said coldly. She sounded idiotic, but she couldn't think straight, her heart pounding along with her head. There were no rules for something like this! When did things like this happen? Never.

"Well, guess what I've been up to?" Beth went on, feeling savage. "I broke up with your boyfriend. I kicked him out, and I'm filing a protective order against him. He can't come near me, or this place."

A long, long silence followed this. Beth glanced at the phone to make sure the call was still connected.

"I'm sorry," she said lamely, which wasn't true.

"Did he hurt you?" Regan said, her voice low and urgent.

"He said he was going to kill me! Regan—how many times has he hurt *you*?"

"He never means it," Regan answered after a long pause. "He just gets so mad."

Beth put a hand to her aching cheek. She wanted to cry. How long had the girl been hiding this? Pretending to the world that her boyfriend was wonderful, they were in love, everything was okay?

"Regan," she said. "He means it. It is not okay for him to treat you like that. It's—"

Her throat closed. These were horror stories Joan told to her and Sherice while they rubbed her shoulders and poured her daquiris. "Honey," Beth tried again. "This is abuse. He is abusing you, and you need to get away from him."

More silence. Beth heard the radio station switch channels.

Beth went to the freezer to look for some ice. There was an ice tray with ancient, withered shards. She poured them into a washcloth and held it to her cheek.

"I didn't know what to do," Beth said as more silence ensued. "I suppose there will be news of it all over the tabloids."

"Eve will know what to do," Regan said. "I'm sorry he hurt you." The radio station flipped again. "He'll come back. He'll apologize. Deep down, he really loves m—you."

Beth sat up. "He won't be coming back in the

next few days. I filed an emergency protective order."

"Shit," Regan swore softly. "He's going to go nuts when he hears that."

"I didn't want to cause you any trouble, I swear," Beth said. "But I was afraid he was going to hurt me. You. Me. And he said he was going to say something about you—"

"I'm sorry, hon," Regan broke in, "but I can't talk about that right now. Are you going to be okay?"

"No." Beth sagged against the bed pillows. "I'm not okay. When is this going to be over?"

"Listen, I have an idea." Her own voice on the line sounded sparkly and determined. "We make the best of it, okay? I'm going to have a great day shopping with Barony. You—just relax. Take it easy. We'll figure everything out, okay? I swear we will."

"We need to find Bene," Beth said. "We need to reverse—whatever this is. Eve said she can get ahold of him."

"Leave Bene out of this," Regan said firmly. "We can figure it out ourselves. Later."

"Not later!" Beth yelled. "We need to worry about it now! I have to teach *Wuthering Heights* on Monday. I haven't talked to my kids in days. I miss my husband." Her throat closed. "I miss my life." She was sobbing out of control now. "I have a great life. I want it back."

"You do have a great life," Regan said. Her voice sounded distant, as if she were looking away. "I promise you, B—babe. I'm going to take care of it. Really good care of it. But I need this right now.

We'll work out our thing later, okay?"

Beth was sobbing so hard she couldn't protest as the call ended. She called back and got the voicemail message that Abby had recorded. "Hi, this is Beth Barony's phone! She's not available right now, but leave her a message, and she'll call you back, okay?"

Beth howled. She wanted to talk to her daughter. She wanted to talk to Drew. She wanted to call Joan, and Sherice, and Barony, and cry on all of their shoulders. But they wouldn't recognize her voice. They wouldn't know who she was, and if she tried to explain it to them, they wouldn't believe her.

Regan Forrester had stolen her life. And Beth had no idea how to get it back.

12 • THE FALLOUT

Beth spent the rest of the morning cleaning the apartment. It was what she did at home when she was having a crisis of any sort, and it was what she did now.

She couldn't call any of her own people, and she didn't know who she could call on here. Regan and her mother didn't appear to be on the coziest terms. Tamara had the day off. And her call to Eve went straight to voicemail. Something fluttered in her belly when she thought about explaining all this to Eve, some memory or experience of Regan Forrester's embedded in her body.

It didn't seem impossible. There were such things as muscle memory, and she had stepped into Regan Forrester's perfectly shaped body, with her lustrous skin, well-toned muscles, delicate bone structure, and her nervous system. Her brain, in fact, but with Beth Barony's consciousness—whatever that was composed of—transplanted into it. Trapped there.

What if Regan Forrester's physical body started absorbing Beth Barony's consciousness? What would happen to her? Who would she be?

She didn't know what to do about Kevin McDonald, or Regan's career, or her own. So she cleaned. It was something concrete of Regan Forrester's life that she could fix.

She started with the bathroom first, gathering everything that appeared to belong to Kevin. Beth couldn't find any plastic totes or cardboard boxes in the apartment, and only one suitcase, a carry-on size roller bag decorated with large purple flowers. But she located a roll of heavy duty garbage bags under the kitchen sink, and they served the purpose. As each bag filled with items, she placed it in the hallway outside the door.

There were several masculine skin products, including a hair tonic that she guessed wasn't working, since the man was bald. As she cleared the medicine cabinet and the cabinet under the sink, she was able to store away Regan's mountain of beauty aids. She organized them by function in the tall, skinny cabinet: hair, body, face. It felt good to have the space clear.

She didn't know what to do with the designer gown she'd worn last evening. It smelled faintly of Timothy Kay's cologne. Beth left it hanging behind the bathroom door and moved into the bedroom.

Kevin McDonald's wardrobe consisted chiefly of several long-sleeved T-shirts, a stack of flannel shirts, jeans with rips in various places, and clunky high-top tennis shoes. The kind of costume he'd worn as a character on that high school sitcom he'd starred in nearly two decades ago.

Regan Forrester couldn't have been in elementary school when that show aired. What did she see in a man so much older than she was?

If she liked older men, it was little wonder she'd thrown herself at Barony. Beth dumped a drawer full of men's briefs into the garbage bag and marched it out the door. Barony was a boxer man.

She couldn't remember what kind of underwear of the men she'd dated before Barony had worn. Barony had replaced every other man, from the moment she'd met him. Sure, they might have gotten in a rut lately, with work obligations, the house to look after, the kids to feed and clothe and drive all over town. But she hadn't looked at another man since they married. She didn't want anyone else.

And now he'd replaced her. Except as far as he was concerned, he was simply sleeping with his wife. Not knowing he was really sleeping with a nubile twenty-four year old, one of *Maxim's* hottest women of the decade, in his wife's stretchy forty-two year-old body. How cheated he'd feel if he knew.

Resolutely Beth started putting Regan's things away in the newly cleared closet and drawers. She unearthed the vanity table, an armchair beneath the window, and an antique dresser with distressed wood. She hung up all the scarves, sorting them by color, and tucked the shoes into a shoe bag that fit inside the closet door.

Regan Forrester had no books in her bedroom, no pictures of family or friends. Beth picked up the one framed photo of Regan and Kevin and hesitated. Regan might want it. She put the picture in the drawer of the nightstand and turned her attention to the rest of the room.

The dish with scattered ashes still stood on the dressing table, next to a white candle, a glass of water, and a small bottle of cloudy blue glass stoppered with a tiny cork. Residue of whatever strange spell Regan had done to achieve this insane body swapping. Beth swept the ashes into a garbage can and tossed the dish in the kitchen sink. She needed to find this Bene and figure out how to reverse the spell.

But there was no number in Regan's phone for a Bene, or anything else that could prove a lead, like, say, a contact labeled Local Practitioner of the Dark Arts or The Little Magic Shop Around the Corner. Maybe she'd find a clue elsewhere in the apartment. Beth finished making the bed and moved into the front room.

First she piled the video game console and all the cords and equipment into a box. Drew would love this system. He'd begged for something like it for his eighteenth birthday.

Beth had hesitated, worried it would interfere with his studies when he started college in the fall. She didn't want him to be one of those young men with so much talent and promise who ended up wasting their lives behind a video game screen.

Barony had accused her of being old-fashioned, but as she filled another box with video games, Beth wasn't so sure. They were all violent war games, military op scenarios, or high-speed escapes from a crime scene.

Many of the covers depicted a preternaturally curvaceous woman wearing little more than pouty lips and clouds of hair. She wanted her son to respect women and consider them equals. She wanted him to be the kind of man who would never hit a woman, nor threaten to hit her. Ever.

Was this video game woman the kind of sexy ideal Regan Forrester was trying to live up to? What a horrific letdown Beth's body must be, in the case. She wondered why Regan hadn't wanted out of it instantly.

Beth's heart squeezed as she started clearing dishes, mail, and other detritus off the dining room table. Barony had put his work aside to take Regan shopping. He hated Mall of America as much as Beth did, but he was spending the day there for her. With her. Beth couldn't remember the last time they'd spent an entire day together. Would he notice anything different?

And dear God, what if this didn't wear off by tomorrow? Regan might be able to distract Barony with sex and giggles, but she could not pull off being Drew and Abby's mother. She couldn't stand in front of Beth's class and pretend to teach.

And what would Dean Chavez say if Regan fell flat on Beth's face in front of an honors seminar of Advanced English Lit students? What if she cost Beth her job? Her salary went into Abby and Drew's college funds, the savings that helped them pay for things like an addition to the house, the IRA she hoped would help keep her and Barony comfortable when they retired.

Beth stifled a sob as she poured hot water into the kitchen sink and started on a pile of dishes. She'd started planning her retirement and her kids' college funds at twenty-three, when Barony joined the law firm and she was pregnant with Drew.

Now she didn't know if she'd have tomorrow, much less see her kids again. What if Drew wasn't enjoying his track team's summer retreat? What if Abby was having a terrible time at band camp? They'd call Beth for advice and get Regan. And today they couldn't call at all because Regan had turned off Beth's phone.

An hour later, the apartment was clean and Beth was hungry. She needed to get out for a while. Especially if Kevin McDonald decided to violate that emergency protective order. What did Regan Forrester do on her days off? Beth had no idea.

So she did what Beth Barony would do. She was the one who'd had her life threatened, after all. She'd get out. Look around. See what she could of LA while she was here. But she was still in Regan Forrester's body, wearing Regan Forrester's face, so for that reason she pancaked foundation over the bruise developing on Regan Forrester's sculpted cheekbone. Then she brushed her hair, pulled on a pair of jeans and a T-shirt, and grabbed her bag. Sandals, sunblock, a pair of dark glasses, and she was out the door.

She'd no sooner stepped onto the sidewalk in front of her apartment building when a man lounging at the bus stop across the street straightened, lifted a camera to his face, and pointed it in her direction.

Beth swore under her breath. The man glanced up and down the street, but traffic was heavy, and the bus approached. Beth picked up her pace, hurrying down the sidewalk.

She wouldn't run. She had nothing to feel guilty about. But she did not want to entertain any questions about why Kevin McDonald had been escorted out of the building this morning by a pair of uniformed LAPD officers. She supposed she couldn't stop them from taking pictures; these were the sorts of things that filled the weekly magazines she thumbed through at the supermarket checkout line, glimpses of celebrities out and about, pretending to have normal lives.

Well, today the paparazzi could take pictures of Regan Forrester buying all of Beth Barony's favorite comfort foods. Beth recalled glimpsing a small grocery store down the street while in Tamara's car.

"Regan? Miss Forrester!" The shout came from behind her.

A street appeared to her right and Beth darted into it, glancing up at a building to note a distinguishing feature. She'd learned this trick from the semester she spent abroad in France: make sure you know how to get back to where you're staying.

The street was a busy pedestrian thoroughfare, crammed with shops, café tables, and vendors selling items from carts and booths. On another day, she'd enjoy walking and browsing, watching people and enjoying the legendary California sunshine. Today she just wanted to hide.

After quite a few zig zags which brought her increasingly away from the trafficked areas, Beth stepped into another alley and at the end of it found a quiet green square filled with huge gnarled oaks and an old fashioned stone church in the center. A line of people snaked out a door to one side.

She'd forgotten it was Sunday. Some people went to church on Sunday. Barony was a lapsed Catholic, Beth had been raised Lutheran but never confirmed, and they hadn't gone to church as a family since the kids grew out of Sunday school and into sports. Beth felt a twinge of guilt at that. Maybe if she were a person of greater faith, something like this would never have happened to her.

A group of people who appeared to be a family stood on the lawn, talking to one another. The women wore colorful head wraps and the men long tunics in vibrant prints. The children played hide-and-seek, laughing. It sounded like they were speaking a sort of French. Tourists? Beth smiled as she neared them. Theirs wasn't the French she taught at the International School, but she could follow it well enough.

"Do you know this church?" she asked in French. If it was their church, maybe they would let her go in. Light a few candles, say a few prayers. Or a hundred.

The elder man turned, his face breaking into a smile. He wore a red cap and there were several white hairs in his beard. One front tooth winked gold. His expression was warm and welcoming.

"We do know this church! Come, today there is a meal." He pointed to the line of people approaching the small church in the center of the square. "Is free. Are you hungry?"

Beth smiled back at him, though she felt guilty and embarrassed. Regan Forrester was an international celebrity, but put her out on the street in LA in her ripped jeans, grubby shirt, and under-fed-looking body, and she looked like someone without home or shelter.

What a sick irony. And Beth *was* hungry at the moment, which was the whole reason she was out here, roaming around, with a starved and lost look on her face.

She couldn't let a reporter catch Regan Forrester standing in line for a free meal. But she and Joan frequently helped Sherice with her church's soup kitchen. There was no more rewarding action than putting food on the plate of a hungry person. No better way to forget her own problems, and Regan's problems, at least for a little while. And no better place than a church to keep Regan's body safe until Beth could figure how to get out of it.

Beth pulled her shoulder bag close, smiling nervously. "Actually, I'd like to help serve the meal. If you'll let me."

13 • THE TEMPLE

Beth's offer of assistance was met with bright exclamations and quick acceptance. One of the women walked with her toward the church. Children scampered at their heels. She took Beth to the kitchen where she washed her hands and helped wrap Beth in an apron, then don a hair net and gloves.

A line of crockpots stood on a front counter and Beth took her place in the row of women doling out bowls of hot stew, slices of bread, and glasses of milk, while the recipients took their trays to sit in the parish hall, which was full of noise and conversation.

The genius of her plan hit her instantly. This was better than cleaning for taking her mind off things. She was in a safe place. She had something to occupy her hands. No one here knew or cared if she were a movie star who made six figures a film or a woman in search of a roof over her head. No one stared, speculated, or tried to take her picture. And with the line of people continuing to snake out the door, there was no time for more than friendly chat with the women she stood next to.

"Where you from?" one of them asked. She wore a set of intricate braids and huge gold hoops in her ears.

"Not too far from here, at the moment," Beth said. "How about you?"

"Inglewood, right now," the woman answered

with a sigh. "But we want to go back to Port-au-Prince as soon as we can."

Haiti, Beth realized. Eve had said that Regan's father was from Haiti. A coincidence, in a city that attracted people from everywhere.

She nodded and kept the chat to a minimum as the line moved, but eventually dwindled. Beth looked up to see the reporter who had photographed her at the bus stop holding out a bowl with a sheepish grin.

"That's some nerve," she said. "Taking charity."

"I put a twenty in the donation box," he said. "And took a picture of you ladling soup. What are you doing here?"

"Hiding from snoopy reporters," Beth said crossly.

He had the cheek to nod his head toward a table. "Join me for an interview? Exclusive?"

"No comment." Beth glared, and he finally moved away.

"He know you?" asked her friend with the earrings as the reporter sat at a table where his was the only white face.

"Of me," Beth said. She hauled the empty crockpot to the sink, following the others. Geez, Regan Forrester was a weakling. For all the time she spent on her body, she wasn't very strong.

"I'm an actor," Beth explained when the woman gave her a questioning look. "I've been in a few pictures." She felt proud saying it, when she ought to have felt stupid. They weren't her pictures. It wasn't her acting skill. But a lot of people dreamed of doing what she did, and she had been lucky—talented, perhaps, but also lucky—to accomplish what she had so far.

Regan, Beth reminded herself with a jolt. Regan Forrester was lucky to be where she was.

Then why didn't she want to be here right now, damn it?

The man she'd seen in the street earlier, the one who invited her in for the meal, came to the counter and praised the women in French. Then he looked at Beth. "You need *hougan*," he said. She guessed now the language they spoke was Haitian Creole, but that word she didn't know.

She glanced for help at the woman who had brought her to the church, the earringed woman who had doled out soup beside her. "Priest," the woman clarified.

"Oh." Beth set her heavy pot on the counter for washing. The bell tower outside and the fixtures within the parish hall suggested that she was in a Catholic church, and she wasn't Catholic. But maybe some prayers would help her. "I think I could use a priest," she admitted.

"Come," he said to the woman, and she nodded and followed, untying her apron. "We need *manbo*," he said to Beth in explanation.

"Priestess," the woman clarified when Beth glanced her way.

Beth might not be Catholic, but she knew the faith did not have priestesses. Her eyes widened as the older couple led her into the sanctuary. The small nave let in light through tall stained glass windows, each depicting a Catholic saint, but below them in the window niches stood candles, beaded ornaments, and platters strewn with leaves and greenery. In each alcove stood a large card with a figure painted on it, all of them dark skinned, some wearing contemporary dress and some traditional garb from West African countries.

The chief difference was the altar. On its delicately embroidered cloth stood candles of all sizes, small statuettes, bottles and jars in many different shapes, small skulls adorned with hats and headwraps, and baskets full of food. Around the altar stood more drums and percussive instruments than Beth had ever seen in one place.

"This isn't Our Lady of Grace any longer, I take it," she said.

The *hougan's* face wrinkled into a delighted smile. Beth felt utterly safe with them, both of them. A warm, calm, joyful spirit pervaded the place, unlike some of the gloomy atmospheres of the Protestant churches she'd known as a child.

"Still belong to *Bondye*, as do all things. The Good God who created us all." He pointed to the ceiling. "But now is temple for the *sèvitè*. We who serve the spirits."

He gestured to the alcoves with their paired figures. As she looked around, Beth saw the women and girls who had helped serve the meal bringing bowls of soup and chunks of bread to lay on the platters before each saint and its companion figure.

The priest's eyes twinkled. "The spirits must be fed. The *lwa* grow hungry in their work."

"Is Vodou, child," the priestess explained. "This is our temple."

"Ah." Beth touched her cheek as the bruise on it ached suddenly. She looked back and forth between the priest and priestess. "I'm—um—not familiar with the—um, practice."

"Not familiar?" the *hougan* barked. "Then how this happen?"

He stepped close and raised a hand toward her face, waiting. When Beth cautiously nodded, the priest took her chin in his fingers. His hands were dry and rough and warm, like her father's hands.

Beth felt a pang of loss. She hadn't called her father in days. He might not notice, busy as he was in the senior living facility he'd moved to after her mom died, but he was her family. Barony. Drew and Abby. Joan and Sherice. They were all her family. Oh, sweet mother, how she missed them.

The priest's face sobered. "I see *ti bon ange* of a wife, mother, a grown woman. But the *gros bon ange* of another." He pronounced it like *gwobonanj.* "A girl."

Beth looked at the priestess. "I don't understand."

"*Gros bon ange* is the big good angel. It comes from our Creator, *Bondye*," the woman explained. She ran a warm, motherly hand down Beth's arm. "You might call it body. That which gives us energy, life. But our sense of *we*, who we are—that is *ti bon ange,* little good angel. The soul."

She shook her head, and her earrings grazed the long, smooth column of her neck. "The two must be tied together." She made a motion of bringing her hands together, drawing them down the front of her body as if closing a zipper. "Vodou helps keep the balance."

"My soul and body are untied." Beth tried to laugh, a short, strangled sound.

The *hougan* nodded. Beth bit her lip. People were still coming in and out, bearing trays of food, adding elements to the altar. She couldn't lose her head and start bawling in front of all these people.

"Where is her *ti bon ange*?" he asked gently. "Departed? In Ginen, the homeland?"

"Not exactly. She's in Minnesota. In my body. My—big good angel." In Beth's house. With her husband, her books, her job, her friends. Beth stifled a howl. "Can you put us back?"

The priest tilted his head as if listening, then exchanged a long look with the priestess. The woman's hands came gently to Beth's shoulders, bracing her for bad news.

"This is not work of *hougan*," the priest said somberly. "Is work of *bokor*." His lips curled as if he tasted something bitter. "Not proper Vodou. Not respect for spirits. Those who want to make the *lwa* serve them."

"What do you mean? What will fix this?"

Beth tried to keep her voice calm. She was not the type to get hysterical. Witness how well she had survived in someone else's body up until now. But cold panic crawled up and down her spine.

"You cannot call the *ti bon ange* back unless you find the *bokor* who has done this." The woman gazed at her with pitying eyes, sensing Beth's distress. "You must find the *lwa* he has called. Only the one who untied the knot can remake it."

"Can't you tell me?" Beth looked around wildly at the quiet, peaceful nave, full of the knowing eyes of the spirits. "Maybe one of these—?" She didn't know what she was talking about, but she was desperate. She'd believe in anything right now if it helped her. Including Vodou.

The priestess's eyes met the priest's. "Each family has its own *lwa*," the *manbo* said with a shake of her head. "They are distinct, like your ancestors. You must speak to the *lwa* you serve. Or she serves." She touched Beth's hand. "Do you know your nation?"

Beth sensed she wasn't talking about a nation as in the sense of the USA. "I don't know her family or her ancestry," she managed. "I only know her father was Haitian. I don't think they're in touch."

"Then *bokor* must undo," the priest said. "You must remember, child. The *lwa* are only messengers of *Bondye*."

"What is a *bokor*?" Beth asked. From the way the elders pronounced the word, she was sure it was not a benevolent entity.

The priest's eyes widened. "What is English word. Magician? He who calls the unhappy spirits. The ones who do mischief and harm."

Beth couldn't stop the tears filling her eyes. "Sorcerer," she said. She bit her lip to hide its trembling. "What happens if he can't fix me?" The cold feeling down her spine had sprouted tentacles that wrapped around her ribs and chest.

The *hougan* looked into the distance and uttered a string of words. They sounded like an incantation.

"We have not seen this before." The *manbo*'s dark eyes were somber, sorrowful. "There are stories, but this—" She paused. "I do not think the *gros bon ange* can go on long. Without the *ti bon ange*, it becomes—a body without a soul."

"*Zonbi*," the *hougan* said ominously.

"Oh, good Lord," Beth choked.

"*Bondye*." The priest nodded, pointing again at the ceiling.

"Is not like your movies," the priestess said with a touch of irritation. "Your Hollywood is very silly. Eating brains? Pffuh." She made a contemptuous sound. "*Zonbi* is form in search of its spirit. It is not how *Bondye* means us to be. When spirit leaves for Ginen, body should be at rest."

"So I'll die if I don't get my soul back in the right body," Beth said.

The priestess shook her head. "Worse than that."

Beth opened her mouth to ask, and then stopped. She could guess the result, and it was more chilling than any of the monster movies Drew loved to watch and then had nightmares about. An animate body, without conscience or will, a slave to whomever controlled it. And where would the soul go, unhoused? Her mind blanked at the thought.

"What if the *bokor* can't fix me either?" she asked in a tiny voice.

"If he cannot help you, we will do what we can. Come back Wednesday." The *manbo* spread out a hand, indicating the serene space around them. "We have service to celebrate Our Lady and Erzulie Dantor. We will pray and dance for you. Perhaps Erzulie Dantor can help. She is protector of women and children, righter of wrongs."

"She can put me back?" But she couldn't wait until Wednesday. She had to teach tomorrow. Beth clasped her shaking hands together.

The priestess laid a hand over the bruise on Beth's cheek. Her touch was cool and soothing, but her eyes were sad. "We will try, child. For her sake, and yours. Erzulie Dantor is very powerful. But we can promise nothing."

The *hougan* shook his head, muttering something in Creole.

"All right." Beth wanted to howl, but she drew a deep breath and recalled her manners. "Thank you—both of you. At least you've given me an explanation. I will find that *bokor* and—I'll be back Wednesday if that doesn't work."

On the street outside the church, Beth stood for a moment, blinking her eyes in the sunshine. The world she'd emerged into from that church was different from the world she'd known before. She'd never known the things they spoke of were possible.

What in God's name had Regan Forrester gotten herself involved in?

She didn't wait till she'd returned to Regan's apartment to send an urgent text to Eve.

I need to find Bene. As soon as possible.

Eve had seemed to know who he was. So did

Kevin, but she wasn't about to ask him for help.

She was nearing the building, anonymous among the busy crowd, when Eve replied. *He's busy tonight. He said get in touch later.*

It's important, Beth texted. Life or death important, but she didn't say that.

Tomorrow night, then. I'll take you.

Monday wasn't soon enough, but at least it was better than Wednesday.

Beth tried calling Regan's mother and left a garbled message. "Listen. I need to know a little more about Dad. Get in touch with him, if that's possible. I hope it's not too weird that I'm asking that. It's important." She paused. "Hope your mouth is feeling better. Maybe you can be my date again sometime, for a better movie."

All the garbage bags with Kevin McDonald's things lay piled in the hallway outside her apartment door. Beth wasn't about to call him to come get them; she didn't want another confrontation. But she didn't know any of his friends who could deliver his things, or get him a message.

She let herself into the apartment and felt a tug at the back of her mind as she entered. Clean, it felt quieter, calmer, more inviting. Almost pretty. There was space to breathe.

It felt strange, though, to be alone. In her real life, she was rarely alone. At school she was either in class or in her office, with other offices surrounding hers and students and administrators and colleagues trooping in and out.

At home, there was always someone coming in and out of the house, Barony or their friends or friends of the kids. She hadn't ever lived on her own, going from her college dorm and roommates to apartments with roommates to an apartment with Barony to their house.

She was embedded in a network of relationships, not just school and home but the many societies she was a part of, the causes she and Barony supported, the local committees they were on. Beth had to schedule when she wanted time to herself.

She sensed that deep down, Regan Forrester was alone.

She couldn't be angry at the girl, knowing that. She put her groceries away, lit a candle, stretched out on the couch, and picked up the phone.

14 • RUNNING LINES

Regan called back while Beth was pressing water out of a square of tofu.

"Hi, honey! How was your day?"

"How was yours?" Beth couldn't keep the rancor from her tone. She was furious at Regan's bright chirp, but something kept her from lashing out. She wondered how much Regan knew of what Beth had learned today. And she wanted to hear what Regan would say about fixing their mix-up. "Had a great time at the Mall of America, did you?"

Regan giggled. "Barony hated it. We came home early." She sounded satisfied. Happy. "He's mixing us drinks. We're going to relax in the Jacuzzi."

"Did you sleep with my husband again?" Beth cried.

"Beth! He's your husband! And it was his idea this time."

"This time!" Beth took a long breath through her nose, something she'd learned in yoga class with Joan. "How many . . . never mind. I can't know that right now. Later, maybe, but not now."

"I bought him a couple of shirts," Regan said, as if that would take away the sting. "And some things for you. Beth! You really need a new wardrobe!"

Beth pounded on the tofu. "Right now," she said, "a new wardrobe ranks at the very bottom of the list of things I need." Whack. "What I *need* is to be in my body—" whack—"in my house—" whack—"sitting in my Jacuzzi"—whack, whack—"while my husband makes me drinks! Which he's terrible at, by the way! He mixes the weirdest stuff. But I would give a lot right now," Beth shouted, "to be drinking Barony's awful screwdrivers, and not worry about finding Bene or some weird sorcerer to reverse this spell, or whatever it is, before my soul comes untethered from my body and floats off into the ether somewhere!"

She squeezed the tofu ferociously until not a drop of liquid emerged. So much for being subtle and laying a trap.

"Tonight," Regan said quickly. "Tonight is your last night of fun. I mean it."

"It wears off tonight?" The anger rose to Beth's throat. "You told me last night that it would wear off, and yet here we are."

"I was wrong. Forty-eight hours, and that's it," Regan said. "That's all the longer it lasts."

Beth clung to the phone. "You mean it? We wake up tomorrow and everything is back to normal? Because if we don't go back—" Her throat closed. She couldn't even say what the priest and priestess at the Vodou temple had told her. Had Regan known what she was getting into? She felt reluctant to put her terror on the girl.

Besides, if Regan wasn't lying this time, she didn't have to worry about seeing Bene and getting him to reverse whatever he'd done. She didn't have to worry about Kevin McDonald walking through the emergency protective order and the apartment door with a gun. She didn't have to worry about anything but fixing a delicious dinner and enjoying every bite of it, and maybe putting on a silky negligee to enjoy Regan Forrester's Frederick's of Hollywood body for one last night.

"Oh, hi, hon. Is that mine?" Regan cooed. "Thanks, babe." A noisy sip. "Sweetie, what is this? It's so good! You are, like, the best drinks maker ever."

"Just tell him it's terrible!" Beth shouted. "Don't praise him for doing something badly! And stop kissing him," she ordered as smacking sounds came over the phone.

Regan giggled. "Okay, come join me soon." Sounds of the porch door sliding shut, then the pad of feet across the porch. A splash, and then a sigh. "Wow, does this feel good. I love your Jacuzzi. I love your house. I love your bed, I love your wine." Another giggle. "I might even start reading your books."

"Don't move any of my page markers in *Wuthering Heights*. I have to teach out of it tomorrow," Beth grumbled.

She prayed she would have a chance to teach tomorrow. Her school, her classroom, her office felt a world away. Like they weren't hers anymore.

"It must be great to be a teacher. Putting knowledge into their little heads. Giving them the skills they need to succeed in life." A swish as Regan dangled her feet in the hot tub.

That sounded like something Beth would say, not something she'd hear from Regan Forrester.

"You wouldn't think that if you had this class. They crucified me over *Northanger Abbey*, absolutely hated it, though it's my favorite Jane Austen novel. And they completely stonewalled me on *Jane Eyre*. I don't think any of them read a word of it. Of *Jane Eyre!*"

Beth flinched to remember how awful those classes had been. They had made her question her worth as a teacher. She'd worked extra hard trying to find passages in *Wuthering Heights* that would be relevant to them, that they could argue and discuss and pull apart as a class. "Maybe things will get better when we get to Dickens. I don't know."

"I think I saw that movie. *Wuthering Heights*. Tom Hardy as the guy, right? Delish."

Beth finished chopping the red peppers and started on the green onions. "You should watch the version with Juliette Binoche. Ralph Fiennes would make me actually choose Heathcliff. Mmm hmm."

Regan laughed. "You wouldn't choose Heathcliff? I thought he was, like, the classic sexy hero."

"I prefer Edgar Linton. The nice, quiet, scholar who is in love with his wife. Witness my choice of husband." Beth's eyes tingled. She blamed the onion.

"I know." Regan sighed. "He's really easy to talk to. And so sweet. It's actually really sexy, how much he loves you, I mean." Regan paused. Was that jealousy in her voice? It was strange, hearing her voice from outside her own head. "He cares what you think. Kevin never asks me what I think about anything."

"Ah. You won't have to worry about that for a

while." Beth moved on to the cilantro, feeling that stab of guilt again. Regan might be threatening her relationship, but she had ended Regan's.

"What, Kevin? He'll come begging for you to take him back. He always does."

"*I'm* not taking him back," Beth said sharply, "and you shouldn't either. I hope you will change the locks and ditch him for good."

"Hmmm." Another long, slow sip. "You know, this tastes fine to me."

Beth pulled the tofu square toward her, then paused. "You want to tell me what Kevin has over you? Some secret you don't want out?"

"It doesn't matter." Regan's voice was lost in another long drink. "I guess it was going to happen sometime. Might as well be now."

Beth put down the knife. The girl's voice tugged at her heart. She wished she could hug her.

And also shake her. She was lying; Beth knew her well enough by now to tell. And Regan Forrester's dissatisfaction with her own life had stolen Beth Barony from hers.

But had she appreciated it? Beth felt another guilty nudge. Had she truly appreciated and valued what she had? Hadn't she been complaining to Joan and Sherice about that vague sense she had of feeling unsettled?

Well, that was nothing compared to this. Being torn out of her life and her body and dumped into someone else's. Even though it was one of the most perfect bodies on the planet, with a gorgeous face. Beth wanted her own body back, with its scars, cellulite, wrinkles, and squishy belly. She would love and honor every inch of that body, once she was back in it. And she would never again complain about her life.

She took a deep breath just as Regan spoke. "Oh! Abby called."

Beth's heart shot into her throat. Her hands trembled so much her tofu squares started coming out uneven. "Abby? She called you? Is something wrong?"

"Calm down!" Regan laughed. "I handled it. She's nervous about the dance that's coming up at the end of the week, after their final performance." Her voice grew muffled for a moment. "Wow, I like this drink. I'm almost done with it."

"What was she nervous about?" Beth barked.

"Oh. Mmm." Another sip. "Well, you know, she has that social anxiety. So I gave her some tricks that I use to get through things like that."

Beth set the knife aside, curling both hands around the phone. "Abby has social anxiety?" She didn't know that. "I mean, I know she's shy, and she gets nervous around strangers, but . . ."

"And that feeling that everyone is judging you, all the time? I used to hide in the bathroom during lunch in middle school so I wouldn't be teased. They would, like, throw ketchup packets at me."

"Abby hasn't done that, has she? She's mentioned that she feels like people are being mean to her, but I . . ."

"Well, *don't* tell her to just get in there and her shyness will wear off," Regan said. "That never works. Trust me."

Beth rubbed her forehead with the back of her hand. Her fingers smelled like onion and tamarind paste. That was exactly what she told her daughter. Beth was a teacher, and before that she'd been in those school plays. She had absolutely no problem with new situations or being in front of people.

"What do I do?"

"We should find her a therapist. And maybe a group. I think a group would be a good start for someone her age."

"We?" Beth said, stung. *She* was Abby's mother. She should have known what her daughter was feeling. What she was fighting. A lump clawed its way up her throat. Regan Forrester had known.

"Oh, and she has a crush on a girl," Regan added. "She was a little freaked out about it. She wondered if she was gay and she'd have to come out and if we'd be upset and stuff."

"She's—what?" Beth leaned both hands on the countertop. Her head spun.

"Well, I don't think she's gay, because she has crushes on boys, too." Regan took another long swallow. Beth's heart pounded in her ears. "I told her it happens all the time. I had all sorts of crushes on girls at her age. I told her not to worry and just enjoy it, because she's probably going to feel attracted to all sorts of people in her life. But also only act on her feelings if it was safe and appropriate," Regan added, sounding motherly.

"That's . . ." Beth pulled out a stool from the dining table and sat down on it. "That's what I would have told her."

"You had crushes on girls, too?" Regan asked curiously.

"Doesn't everyone? But I never . . . and anyway, Abby is way too young to be having sex!" Beth said. "But I can handle crushes. As long as Abby is okay and not upset about it."

"She seemed fine after we talked."

Beth put a hand over her heart. She wasn't sure that she *would* have been so calm and wise with Abby. She was her mom. Abby's every upset went straight to Beth's gut.

"I'm . . ." Beth drew in a deep breath. "I'm glad she had you to talk to. Thank you, Regan." Tears smarted her eyes. *She* was Abby's mom. *She* wanted to be listening to and helping and consoling her daughter.

"She's really great, isn't she?" Regan said this with a touch of loving pride, as if she'd had a part in making the girl. "I love how she can talk to you. I can't talk to my mom about anything."

"I got that impression," Beth said. She hesitated. "What about your dad?"

"Gone," Regan said shortly. Her voice rose suddenly. "Hey, babe, are you coming out? Want to bring me a refill?"

"Don't drink too much," Beth said, alarmed. "I have to teach tomorrow. I don't want to be hungover. And if you're on the porch, Mrs. Henderson can see you."

"Maybe I'll invite her over." Regan giggled. "I think she's lonely. She's got a thing for Barony."

"Mrs. Henderson? What?"

"You've got to watch out for him, Beth! He's a catch. Women eye him all the time. I had to peel one of the salesladies off him at the mall today."

"Off of *Barony*?" Beth said, profoundly surprised.

"Have you forgotten what he looks like?" Regan said sternly. "Do I need to send you a picture?"

"I know what he looks like," Beth snapped. "Of course I think he's gorgeous. It's just . . . I didn't think he was gorgeous to anyone else. Because I see him with the eyes of love."

"Well, other women are looking at him with the eyes of lust," Regan said, "so someone needs to stake her claim, girlfriend."

"Not you," Beth riled. "Me. I'm going to be back in my body any minute now." Anger flashed through her chest.

"Hey, babe! Back so soon?" Regan trilled. "Do you think we should invite Mrs. Henderson over? She's, like, falling over the fence to see you in your swim trunks."

"Regan!" Beth shouted. "Stop flirting with my husband!"

"So, tomorrow is class, and the meeting with the dean," Regan said loudly. "And then I'm going out with Joan after work. We invited Sherice, but she's working a double shift, so she can't come."

Beth guessed by the change in her voice that Barony had joined her on the deck. She *had* to be home tomorrow. She couldn't let Regan in the room with Dean Chavez. The woman was her boss as well as a friend.

"Me," she growled. "That's *my* day tomorrow. *I* teach my class. *I* get together with Joan."

"One last night of freedom!" Regan chirped.

Then she made another sound, a sort of soft sigh. Beth's heart clenched.

"Stay away from my husband! You've had enough!"

"No worries," Regan purred. "We're just going to dip in the pool . . . mmm . . . and sip some wine . . . mmm! And maybe be a *little* bit naughty." She gave a throaty chuckle.

"Just don't get drunk and pass out in the tub," Beth snapped. "Or let Mrs. Henderson see what you're doing. She could get me fired, you know."

"Hi. Beth has to go now." Suddenly Barony was speaking into the phone. "She's got plans for the night."

"Barony." Beth clutched the phone, her chest aching. Something hot and hard pressed at her throat. "God, it's good hear your voice."

But the little beep told her the call was over.

Beth put her head in her hands, shaking. Hearing her husband's voice was the tipping point for the day's surprises. She'd been on edge, wary, frightened all day. She didn't know where to turn, where she was safe, and here was Regan Forrester enjoying Beth's Jacuzzi while giving advice to Beth's daughter, making friends with Beth's neighbors, and making passionate and repeated love to Beth's husband. In Beth's body, true, but it was Regan who was getting to enjoy him, not Beth. She felt too frightened to cry.

What if Regan was lying again? What if this had no end?

No, there was an end. The Vodou priest and priestess had explained to her. If she didn't unite her soul with her proper body, it might float away. She might be stuck in Regan Forrester's perfect body for the rest of her natural life, or be an unhoused spirit for the rest of time, roaming the earth keening for the life she had lost. Either result sounded like eternal hell.

A knock on the door sent a bolt of fear through her heart. Kevin, come to get his things. What if he threatened her again?

"Who is it?" she called, trying to steady her voice.

"Salesman," came the deep reply. "For home security systems. Heard you could use one."

She opened the door to the tall, powerful form of Timothy Kay.

15 • THE DINNER

A whisper of warning lifted the hair on Beth's neck. This man was dangerous. She hadn't been attracted to another man since she met Barony.

Barony, who was at this moment ravishing the woman he thought was his wife, who had somehow reacquired the libido she'd had in their early twenties, before childbirth and child rearing. He wouldn't question how it happened. No doubt he was simply delighted by the gift.

Beth unhinged the chain and opened the door. "Come in."

"You're alone?"

His eyes glanced around the area. How glad she was that she'd cleaned, a few candles burned on the table, and soft music played from an enormous entertainment system. No doubt that was Kevin's, too, and he'd insist on having it. She'd give it to him. She'd give him anything if he would leave Regan alone, set her free from whatever hold the man had over her.

"I find that surprising," Timothy said.

Beth rubbed her nose, which still tingled with threatening tears. "That I'm home? Or that I'm alone?"

"I thought you had a—roommate."

Again he scanned the room, bare of anything that suggested masculine habitation, in fact rather bare overall. Once she'd heaped up Kevin's things, Beth had tucked away much of the remaining clutter, leaving a calm, quiet, inviting space in the apartment. It looked more like the home of an adult rather than the landing pad for a confused adolescent. Beth opened the door wider, not ashamed for him to see it.

"My roommate's moving out."

"Oh." Timothy glanced at the piles of garbage bags. "I thought maybe that was for charity. Since you have a community service streak I apparently didn't know about."

Beth turned away and headed back to the stove as he stepped into the room and closed the door. "Does someone report to you on my every move?"

"Only because our movie just opened, so everything is about promotion right now."

The room felt small, more intimate with him in it. His cologne drifted to her nostrils, and a slow, deep heat uncoiled in her belly. He walked around the room, examining the art on the walls, old movie posters and vintage prints of pin-up girls. Not terribly classy. "So this is your place," he said.

"I don't know where the money goes," Beth said honestly. It puzzled her why Regan, who had instant name recognition, lived in such a shabby apartment. Maybe she preferred it. Maybe she was supporting her mother. Maybe there was something Kevin was holding over her. Beth opened and shut cabinets until she found glasses.

"Do you want wine? I picked up a Riesling to go with the pad Thai."

His eyebrows rose. "You're making dinner?"

"And you find that surprising as well."

"I didn't know you cooked. Or drank."

He accepted the glass she poured, and their fingers touched. She drew away.

"You don't seem to know me very well."

It was a flippant response. He couldn't know her; he'd never met Beth Barony in her life. She ought to remember she was in Regan Forrester's skin.

Actually, she *did* remember she was in Regan Forrester's skin, because Timothy Kay's eyes moving over her was a potent reminder, even though she wore the ripped jeans and worn T-shirt that she'd served soup in. She'd found them in the back of the bottom drawer of the dresser.

From her Internet search and the looks of her closet, Regan Forrester worked the sexpot, take-me-now look all the time, even in her off hours. It had to be exhausting to be that image of perfection. Beth couldn't pull of the sexpot look even in this body, and wasn't about to try.

Timothy Kay's assessment made a prickle move over her skin. He knew more about Regan Forrester than she did. He was judging her level of hotness right now, she'd bet. Re-evaluating whether she was sexy enough to be in his next movie.

She'd like to toss him out on his ear if that were the case, but she ought not to risk Regan Forrester's career. Even if the girl was at this very moment sipping wine in Beth's hot tub and wrapping herself around Beth's husband. At least she was in Beth's body. Was that cheating, technically speaking? It sure felt like it.

"You didn't hang out a lot on set. You had your

earbuds in between takes, and you never went out with the cast and crew. You always said you had to get home to Kevin."

Who no doubt hated Regan being out of his control. Had she been happy with him? Was she going to take him back when Beth was gone?

"Well, I got out today." She poured a generous glass of wine for herself and sipped. The cool, dry wine nipped at her tongue, awakening her senses.

"Do you do this a lot?"

"Cook?" She lifted her eyebrows. "Yes." Nearly every night. Family dinner was a ritual she and Barony insisted on. Even when the kids were running in two separate directions, they ate together as often as they could. No phones, no electronic devices, no homework, no distractions. They had to talk to one another, and listen.

Who in her life listened to Regan Forrester?

"Help serve free meals at church soup kitchens on Sundays." Timothy leaned one lean hip against the kitchen counter, observing her mise en place.

"It was my first time around here," Beth admitted, though serving community meals was something she did all the time. She often helped out at Sherice's church, and several times a year she helped Joan organize fundraisers where people cooked food for the domestic violence shelter.

She noticed, though, as she got out the large frying pan that would have to serve as her wok, coated it with oil, and turned on the heat, that she had to concentrate on what she was doing. The movements weren't habitual anymore. Something

Beth Barony did automatically wasn't coded into Regan Forrester's muscle memory. She hoped the dish would turn out. Pad Thai was her comfort food, a treat that always made her feel better.

"Are you staying for dinner?"

He looked at her over the rim of his glass. His eyes looked dark from afar, but up close they were a deep brown shot through with gold streaks in the iris. Cat's eyes. That warning wafted over the back of her neck again.

"I was going to see if you wanted to go out for dinner. But you've already begun."

She pulled a second plate from the cupboard and handed it to him. "You can set the table."

Regan Forrester had purely functional dinnerware, the kind of thing Beth had bought for her first apartment, nothing like the heavy decorative dishes she'd acquired since she married. Regan's silverware was cheap and she had no placemats, no chargers, no cloth napkins, no linens for the table whatsoever. Timothy Kay didn't seem to notice or care. He laid out two place settings, side by side. Beth focused on searing the tofu.

"You're sure you and Kevin broke up." He was back at her side, so tall, looming over her shoulder. His body heat warmed her arm. Beth jumped. "He seems the jealous sort."

"He'll have to get over it," Beth snapped. "I got an emergency protective order."

Timothy let out a low whistle, his brows climbing his face. What a handsome face he had, lean cheeks, well-defined jaw, dark lashes spiking his eyes. His hair was shaggy and in need of a cut—Barony never let his hair get too long—but he'd recently shaved.

For the first time she noticed he was wearing a dark T-shirt, a suit jacket, and a pair of dark slacks with loafers. Not a Hollywood power suit, by any means, but something he could take out to a classy restaurant. He *had* come over to invite her on a date.

Or rescue her. The thought made her neck warm.

"Did you talk to Eve? She's going to want to do some sort of damage control."

"I didn't tell her yet." She had more important things to focus on with Eve. Like finding Bene. "Why?" Beth glanced up at his face. "Worried this will affect the movie?"

"Eve will want to work up a statement for the public."

He watched her with those dark eyes. Tiny hairs on her shoulders lifted. The priest and priestess from earlier had looked at her and known something was wrong. Did anyone else see it?

"Of course." Beth prodded tofu pieces with her spatula. "Can't have something like an abusive boyfriend spoiling the public image."

Timothy frowned. "How abusive?"

"He made threats. Said there's something he knows about—something he could tell people."

Her stomach turned over. Regan's body reacted in fear at the thought of Kevin, at the very mention of his name. It was hard for Beth to think logically around that.

"I don't care how that reflects on the movie," Timothy said sharply, as if guessing her thoughts. "I care about your safety."

"And that I'll be in one piece for filming *Visitors 2*."

"Hey." His hand curled around her wrist. His fingers were strong and warm. His low voice curled around her ear, sending fissures down the length of her spine. "Tell me what you need."

Oh, so many things. Her husband. Her friends. Her life back. Before Regan Forrester put her relationship with her kids, or her job, or her status in the neighborhood at risk.

"The tamarind paste," Beth said shakily. "It's right there. Want to hand it to me?"

Dinner with Timothy Kay wasn't a move toward safety. She felt his heat, smelled his scent as she brought the tray of steaming noodles to the table. He poured them a fresh glass of wine. The music, a low, jazzy croon, drifted through the dim, quiet lights of the apartment. There was no noise of a city outside, no sirens, no shouting, no traffic. The hallways of the building were quiet as well. They sat in a warm island, adrift from the rest of the world. Her real life felt further away than ever.

"This is delicious."

Timothy dug into his plate, relishing it. Beth couldn't remember the last time Barony or the kids complimented her cooking. More often they shoveled it in their mouths, talking a mile a minute, and then were running off to practice, study group, or in Barony's case his office to get some more work done for the evening. It was so nice to have an intimate dinner and conversation with an adult.

Beth tried a mouthful and then put down her fork, frowning. "It tastes different."

"What do you mean?"

"I made it the same way I always make it, exactly the same, but—" It didn't taste good to her. This was her comfort dish and she'd meant to stuff herself with it, but Regan Forrester's taste buds spoiled it. Just as Regan had spoiled everything else of Beth's.

She wanted to cry.

"It's terrific."

"It's edible." Beth reached for her wine glass. "So, what else is coming up for you, besides this sequel?"

He told her. The conversation was easy, unguarded. Timothy Kay was charming and clever. Never mind that the longer she watched him eat, enjoying her food, the more Beth felt heat building in her belly. Was this something Regan Forrester had felt, this physical draw to her director, or was the attraction Beth's, the admiration she felt for an accomplished, interesting man?

He wasn't the person she assumed he was based on the movie he'd created. It seemed the producers and the studio were responsible for the explosions, the noise, the massive special effects. He'd wanted a story with more room for the characters' emotions, and a more complex theme about environmental destruction and the enemies a state creates through violence and wars. He'd taken on a script for what he thought was a psychological thriller, where the aliens played a metaphorical role, and had been railroaded by the studio into making a film where good and evil were clearly marked, his characters were stereotyped, and the aliens were little more than destructive machines with a genocidal agenda and an opportunity for the CGI programmers to go overboard.

"Maybe, if the film does well, they'll give you more creative license in the sequel," Beth said.

She'd managed to eat part of her plate of pad Thai, but it was disappointing. She didn't feel the cozy rush of comfort she'd anticipated. Instead, she felt bitter and over-full. Regan Forrester's body wasn't used to carbs.

"That's my hope." He pushed his empty plate aside and regarded her. "In fact, that's what I came by to talk to you about. I've been giving some thought to the suggestions you made yesterday."

"You have?" Beth blinked. "That was fast."

"And I got some ideas from your photo shoot."

"It's live already? That was *really* fast."

"I told you, the reporter contacted me for comments. She also sent a couple of the images."

He tapped his phone and turned the screen toward Beth. There was Regan Forrester, draped in filmy white that added a deep luster to her tawny skin and sable hair. The nearly sheer material clung to her form, outlining the corset that pushed up her breasts, skimming the length of one long, shapely leg. Her hair floated as if lifted on the wind and her expression, musing and distant, suggested her mind was roaming in far distant imaginative fields.

There was nothing overtly suggestive in the slight pout of the lip, the classic curve of the cheek, or the wistful postures the photographer had put her in, but the overall effect was incredibly appealing, combining fairy tale enchantment with the secretive, shadowed wisdom of a mature woman.

Beth sucked in her breath. It was Regan Forrester's body, and yet she felt she was looking at herself. Noting every flaw, every imperfection, every hint of awkwardness, the hints of a woman not comfortable in her own skin. How could she be comfortable in that skin? It wasn't *hers*.

She looked away from the haunting photos. "I like the waif look way better than the sexpot."

Timothy's eyes were dark and smoky. "Me, too." He slipped the phone into his jacket pocket. Beth tried not to notice those deft, long-fingered hands. "Want to come to the studio with me? I'm trying to get some set ideas to send the designer."

"Do you mean, go out?"

His lips curved with amusement. Best not to notice those perfectly shaped lips, either. "Yes, going to the soundstage would entail leaving here."

A thread of nervousness, odd and unprecedented, tugged at Beth's stomach. She wasn't nervous in new scenarios. She got thrown into new scenarios at least once a semester. Social anxiety was Regan Forrester's thing. Beth was glad for a reason to leave the apartment; she didn't want to be around when Kevin came for his things.

"Ok. Just let me change and wash up."

She slid off the stool. She was aware of Regan's body again, lithe and supple. Beth Barony would never flow off a bar stool, but Regan Forrester did.

"Tell you what. I'll clean up while you change."

Timothy stacked their plates and put their forks on top.

Beth stared at him. "You do dishes?"

"When a woman cooks for me, yes. Is that so shocking?"

"A little. My hu—my—roommate hates doing dishes. I have to bribe and threaten." She'd stumbled on the word husband. It felt foreign on her lips.

She had a husband. Barony. In Regan Forrester's arms. Were they done by now, or indulging in some long love-making marathon? Beth was conscious of a swing to her hips as she walked to the bedroom. Beth Barony never swung her hips, but Regan Forrester did by instinct.

She didn't plan to get dolled up, just get out of the grubby jeans that she'd cooked and cleaned and served soup in. It wasn't a date. She was simply getting out of the apartment.

But as she studied the rows of colorful fabric hanging in Regan Forrester's closet, Beth felt a wicked impulse curl through her chest. Regan Forrester had some adorable clothes. Regan Forrester had the body to make them look good. It seemed a shame to waste an opportunity, since she had one more night in this costume, to enjoy the feeling of a clingy dress on a taut, toned body.

She chose a sleeveless, silky green number with a floor-length skirt that brought out the green of Regan's eyes. It was adorned with a few silver spangles, but nothing overly fancy, and the neck-line, though deep, only hinted at cleavage. She found a pair of strappy silver sandals to match.

Hair and makeup were more daunting; Regan Forrester owned enough cosmetics to start her own counter, while Beth was never the type to waste time grooming. A dab of mascara, a slide of lip gloss, a brush through her hair, and she was done. She liked Regan Forrester with a more natural, relaxed look, a hint of freckles, her eyes sparkling instead of sultry, her lips smiling instead of pouting.

The only perfume she saw was a label Beth hated and thought smelled like turpentine. But when she uncapped it, the scent that hit her nose was subtle but heady, like the loamy background of a tropical garden, a bit dizzying, very warm. She had Regan Forrester's nostrils, Regan Forrester's taste buds. The slide of the silky fabric over her smooth skin gave Beth a rush she'd never felt before.

It was Regan Forrester's body responding to the potent, masculine charisma of Timothy Kay. It wasn't Beth cheating on her husband. Not really.

She came out of the bedroom carrying a small clutch and found him, sleeves rolled up to his elbows, wiping his hands on a towel. A stack of dishes gleamed on the drying rack, the stovetop was clean, and the leftovers had been put away.

Beth stared at the flexing muscles in his forearms. She had to resist this attraction. He had the power to short circuit her brain.

He stared back, his voice deepening. "You look like I should take you dancing."

Beth smiled, a flirtatious, seductive smile. *Stop flirting!* "I haven't been dancing since the wedding," she said, which sounded so terribly, terribly sad. She loved dancing. Why had she stopped?

Once again that inquisitive brow was on the move. "The wedding?"

"Umm. The wedding for a friend. I was at recently." She forced a bright smile. "Gold star for dish duty. You even wiped the stove."

"I'm actually domesticated." He pulled on his jacket and Beth shamelessly watched the ripple of muscle across his shoulder. Such broad, firm shoulders he had. "Don't tell anyone."

That odd shiver moved over her again as he opened the door. When had a man last opened a door for her? He held the way open to something new that hadn't been possible for her before. Freedom. Adventure. The challenge of a new project, a new job. An entirely new world she didn't know existed.

"Let me guess. Hollywood director. Rich. Single. You've got a line of women at your door twelve deep."

He pulled her apartment door shut behind them, turned it to make sure it was locked. Checking on her safety again. A delicious thrill moved through her body, and when his hand came to her lower back, possessive, exploratory, a bright warmth blossomed under his touch.

She hadn't felt this kind of arousal in so, so long. She was a married woman. Her desires were sated regularly, at least once a week, once every other week if Barony was exhausted from work or out of town. She'd forgotten the anticipation of not knowing if someone wanted her back. She'd forgotten the delirium of being on the scrumptious cusp of something, wondering if she ought to pursue it, wondering what might unfold at any moment.

What had Regan said to Abby about her crush? *Enjoy it.* While Regan was freely enjoying Beth's husband. Very well, she would have her revenge.

She spent the evening with Timothy Kay, charming, clever, sinfully handsome Timothy Kay. They talked about the script and costumes as they moved across the vast empty soundstage, while he painted the movie for her in words and gestures.

She let that thrill slide around her body, weave in and out of her belly, light up her forgotten depths. She smiled inside every time his hand brushed Regan Forrester's body or lifted a lock of hair out of her face. She sighed inside every time he spoke near her ear and gooseflesh broke out over her back. She licked her lips, at least on the inside, when she caught an odd, riveted look in his eye that made her nipples harden and her breath catch.

And when he kissed her outside her apartment—kissed Regan Forrester, that is, outside of Regan Forrester's apartment—she clamored and cheered and did cartwheels on the inside, because his mouth was so warm and his lips were so sensuous and his tongue was so skilled, and she didn't stop his hands from sliding down her dress, and she let her own hands thread though his hair, which was as soft beneath her fingers as his body was hard against her.

They kissed for what felt like hours, a delirium of desire, a litany of lust, and when she stumbled into bed, alone, Beth didn't even try to stop the satisfied smile that spread over her face, even though the body she was in hummed with unsatisfied desire.

She'd enjoyed it thoroughly, the cusp, the promise, the delicious sense of what was possible. The thrill of the new and unknown, something she hadn't known for two decades and would never know again.

She could forgive Barony, now, for adoring another woman in her body, when she could clutch this secret to her chest. She'd kiss Barony awake tomorrow morning and spend this pent-up desire on him, her husband. She'd made the most of her time as Regan Forrester. She had no regrets.

Until she turned over the next morning and saw the beaded lamp, the purple cellphone, the candle on her dresser with the evaporating glass of water and the bitter last trace of herbs. She was still in Regan Forrester's body, Regan Forrester's home, Regan Forrester's bed, Regan Forrester's life.

While Regan still had Beth's life, Beth's husband, Beth's cat at the foot of the bed.

And, in less than an hour, Beth's class to teach.

Beth leapt out of bed and grabbed the phone.

16 • CLASS PREP

"Okay." Beth took a deep breath. *Think, Beth, think.* "We can fudge this for today. Just have them watch the movie and write about—something. About how the setting and the natural elements reflect the emotions of the characters."

"They really do!" Regan exclaimed in Beth's disembodied voice. Beth heard her open the bathroom door, start running the tap. Regan Forrester brushed Beth's teeth with Beth's toothbrush while Chester, no doubt twining himself around her ankles, yowled to be fed. "All the wild moors and stuff, it just seemed so lonely. But a movie, Beth?" Regan said with her mouth full of toothpaste. "That's so lame."

"Everybody loves movie day," Beth protested. "Movie day is the best."

"Movies are a crutch, and we know it." Some muffled sounds followed. "We want to talk about the ideas. We want to examine the characters."

"*I* want to talk about the ideas," Beth said irritably. "I want to examine the characters. My students are just going to complain that Cathy is a whiny spoiled princess and Heathcliff is so sexy and brooding. If they talk at all." She reflected on the last two weeks, the many bored silences. She, an experienced teacher, hadn't been able to make this class gel. They were going to eat Regan Forrester alive.

"Sexy? As if!" Regan spat. "He's, like, an abuser. He's so damaged and mean, and he suffocates her. He basically drives her to suicide."

"She starves herself to death to spite him and Edgar both, and because she doesn't want to give up her girlhood and become a mother," Beth argued. "And a lot of women love that dark and damaged bit."

Regan rinsed. "Maybe that's why I put up with Kevin."

Beth didn't want to talk about Kevin McDonald. He added to the sour feeling rolling in Beth's guts. She went to refrigerator and pulled out leftovers.

"Look, I'm trying to help you get through the day. The movie and the in-class essay. The DVD is downstairs on the shelf next to the entertainment center. The smartboard is easy to run, the kids will tell you how to do it. Just get through the day and I'll be back tomorrow, and I can fix everything then."

"What do you mean, you'll be back tomorrow?"

Beth paused and flinched as the scent of cold pad Thai hit her nostrils. She loved pad Thai! What was wrong with her? Was Regan Forrester going to take every last thing away from her, including her comfort foods?

"I'm going to see Bene tonight. Eve is taking me." As a silence pooled, she added, trying to rein in her tone, "I made a backup plan. In case, you know, this didn't wear off like you'd thought."

More silence ensued. Footsteps sounded from the other end of the phone, the click of the kitchen tiles. How she missed her kitchen, the long marble top counters, the gleaming appliances, the space. She heard the scrape of the food bowl, and Chester stopped yowling.

"Beth, I wish you would have a little faith in me. I can *do* this. I can teach your class." She heard rummaging sounds.

"I hate to pull rank here, but I have a master's degree in English education. And you?"

"I have a GED." Regan sounded defensive. "I got it while I was working the soap opera after Mom moved us to LA. And besides, I read the book."

Beth heaped pad Thai onto a plate and slammed the door to the microwave. "You read *Wuthering Heights.*"

"Well, it's right here on your nightstand, with all your notes and underlining, and I read some of it on the drive yesterday, and then last night after—" A brief pause. "After Barony went to sleep."

After Regan exhausted him with passionate and no doubt wildly inventive love-making the likes of which he had never known. How disappointed Barony was going to be when he got his real wife back.

"Your notes are really good," Regan added when Beth said nothing. "They got me questioning some things I hadn't thought about."

"Yes, that is the point. That is what we teachers like to do." Beth closed her eyes.

"So! Teacher!" A drawer slammed, and silverware clinked against the countertop in Beth's kitchen. "What's my goal for this scene?"

"This is not an acting job, Regan," Beth moaned. "This is my career."

She rotated the plate in the microwave and added another thirty seconds. "Your goal is to not get me fired."

"I think I can come up with better motivation that *that*," Regan said. A sound of crunching filled the phone. "I want to expand their minds. I want them to consider how other people lived in other times and places." More crunching. "I want them to consider how this, like, really old book might mean anything in our day."

"Those are the reasons I became an English teacher," Beth said distractedly. "Are you eating toast?" She carried the hot plate to the dining table, grabbing a fork.

"Mmm-hmm. Beth!" Regan said after she swallowed. "Your body loves carbs. I can't eat them at all, but they make you *so* happy." Her voice sharpened. "What are *you* eating? I can hear you slurping."

"Carbs," Beth said around a mouthful of noodle. "You're right, your body hates them. My stomach hurts so much this morning. But I can't stop." She shoveled in another mound of noodles. "How can you not like Thai food? I could have cried when I made this beautiful dish and could barely eat it. At least Timothy enjoyed it."

"Timothy?" The sound of chewing stopped. There was a dramatic silence on the other end of the phone.

"Umm. Your director, Timothy Kay. He stopped

by when he heard—ah, that Kevin was moving out, and—I invited him to stay for dinner. Since I already had something started."

Now why should she feel guilty? Because she'd enjoyed his company, enjoyed the attraction? Because she'd kissed him with delirious pleasure in her hallway for what felt like ages? Well, Regan and Barony had gone much further. Still, her stomach writhed.

"Don't put that in my body, Beth! I'm on a very special diet. The green liquid only."

Beth groaned. "It smells terrible. How can you eat that?"

"It's something one of Kevin's friends designed. He arranged it all and has portions delivered each day. I promised to try it and be the spokesperson when he tries to sell it."

"Well, I'm destroying your body with carbs and alcohol," Beth said. "Come take it back and stop me."

"Are you working out at all?" Regan cried. "You'll get fired from the *Visitors* sequel if you get fat and out of shape! The producers already told Eve they thought I was too heavy."

"Are you kidding me?" Beth yelped. "Regan, you are a popsicle stick with boobs."

"Excuse me!" Regan exclaimed. "I am *Maxim's* hottest woman of the year."

"*I* am Maxim's hottest woman of the year," Beth said smugly. Now where had that come from? It wasn't like her to be malicious. "*You* are a Midwestern mom on the cusp of middle age. Any minute now you'll start menopause."

Another silence followed this, and then Regan spoke in a strange voice. "You know, I hadn't thought of this before, but Beth, are you on birth control? Because there's been a lot of . . ." She trailed off.

"I'm on the pill." Beth clenched the phone, putting down her forkful of noodle. "Which, let me guess, you haven't been taking."

"Well, how was I to know? I've got an implant. And it's not like you reminded me," Regan accused her.

"Do not get my body pregnant!" Beth yelped. "We don't want more kids! Barony and I both agreed we'd stop at two. I don't want another baby. I'd be sixty years old when it graduated high school."

"I want kids. Lots of kids," Regan said dreamily. "At least four, I think. How could you stop at just two?"

"Because I only have two arms," Beth snapped. "Regan, whatever you do—do not have a baby with Kevin. He is so, so not good for you."

"I know." Regan nibbled at the last of her toast. "I should have kicked him out a long time ago. Thanks for doing it for me."

"You can thank me by not getting me pregnant." Beth put a hand on her stomach as nausea hit. Regan Forrester's body really did not like carbs. "Or getting me fired. Or making Joan mad when you see her later. Or giving me a tattoo."

"Seriously, what is it with you and tattoos? They're not that scary." Regan sounded amused.

"Whoops, there's another call—wait a sec—" She came back on the line.

"Who's Drew?"

"My son." Beth's heart pounded. "He's at track camp. Let it go to voicemail."

"Why don't you want to talk to him? What if he needs me?"

"Needs *me*," Beth cried, "and I don't want him to guess something's wrong. Let it go to voicemail and I'll call him back."

"I gave Abby good advice," Regan said indignantly.

"You did. Thank you." Beth realized she needed to take a different tack. "And I'm sure you'll do great with my students today. You'll be brilliant. If things get rough, just dismiss them early. Say you got sick. Push back my meeting with Dean Chavez. I'll smooth everything over tomorrow."

The nausea climbed up her chest to her throat. Beth feared she would throw up. If she had a tomorrow. "This will all be over by tomorrow."

A pause followed. "Drew left a voicemail." Regan sounded subdued. "I feel guilty about that."

"Me, too." Beth pushed her plate away.

"You know, it's strange." She heard a chair move, and then Chester's rumbling purr came over the line. Her cat hadn't noticed Beth was missing, either.

"When your kids call," Regan said softly, "or I'm around Barony, or Joan—I feel this . . . pull. It's like your body holds your love for them. And their love for you. It's really . . ." She paused. "It's really nice."

Beth put her head in her hands.

"Now imagine being away from them for three days. When you love them and you know they need you, and you can't be there."

"But see, I don't have that. People just make me nervous. I'm always worried they're judging me. I'm scared about what they think. It's so hard. At least with Kevin—well, he helped keep it all away, at least in the beginning. So I didn't have to deal with so much."

Suddenly, Beth understood. Kevin had isolated Regan so he could control and manipulate her, because that's what abusers did. But to Regan, he had felt like a safety net.

And Beth had torn that safety net away from her.

A few days ago, she would have said she didn't know what Regan was talking about—that feeling of not quite being safe around people, not sure she was accepted. Never feeling she was loved. Beth might have had her own dissatisfactions or worries, but she had never doubted the strength of her relationships.

She would have said, four days ago, that Regan Forrester was the most confident, self-possessed, self-assured woman alive. But after living three days in her body, with this nervous jumpiness in her stomach at the thought of what the day held, she understood.

Who could she trust? Who could she rely on? Who loved her for her and wasn't just using her to get ahead?

"Oh, hey!" Regan's voice sounded bright again. "I

found the cutest outfit yesterday for you to wear teaching. I'm going to wear it today. Want me to send you a picture?"

"No, do not send me a picture of my body. My head might explode," Beth said. "You bought clothes for me?"

"Mmm-hmm. Told you you needed a wardrobe overhaul. And this one I thought, I'd feel so confident teaching in. It's just the right look."

"You teaching," Beth repeated. "You planned this? You expected this?" Her voice rose. "You knew this wouldn't wear off?"

"Um." Regan's voice was muffled, like she was pulling fabric over her head.

"What else are you not telling me?" Beth shouted. "What's going on, Regan?"

"I'm going to go teach *Wuthering Heights*," Regan chirped. "I'm kind of excited about it. And I look hot! All the boys are going to have a crush on you, Beth."

"Because let me tell you what I know," Beth blazed on. "I learned quite a bit yesterday about Haitian Vodou. I looked it up online. It's different from Louisiana Voodoo, which I'm sure you know, and nothing like what's presented in the movies. There's a very interesting philosophy about spirits called *lwa*. It's quite beautiful in some ways. All about tuning into a bigger world than we can imagine."

"Beth, honey, Barony's calling to wish me luck. We'll talk about this later, okay? Don't worry about anything. Tamara has your day all mapped out."

"I have one plan for my day," Beth shouted into the phone. "Find Bene and reverse this. Because you know what happens if we don't? Do you know what will happen to me? To us? We turn into—"

"Goodbye!" The green line of a live call blipped away.

"Zombies!" Beth shrieked at the silent device. "We turn into zombies!"

The phone vibrated with a text message just as she was about to hit the call button. She hoped it was Regan explaining herself. The girl had to talk to her.

The title on the little text balloon said "Kevin."

The text inside said *You want to play? Bring it, bitch.*

She followed the link to the website and was staring at it in horror when Tamara knocked on the door.

17 • THE INTERVIEW

Mechanically Beth went to the door, pulled back the deadbolt, and unhooked the chain. She held the phone in one hand, still staring at the screen.

". . . so her mother's an alcoholic, like, completely bombed out of her mind all the time."

Kevin sat on the blue couch across from the interviewer, who perched behind his desk in the same argyle sweater vest, thick-framed glasses, and severely gelled hair he'd worn in the interview with Regan.

"So that's part of the reason for her problem with prescription drugs. And her father, wow, he's a piece of work. He bailed back to Haiti when she was five or something, so she has insane relationship issues over that." Kevin glanced at the camera with a smug "take that" expression.

"Sounds like a hot mess!" the interviewer exclaimed. "Tell us more. Nothing is TMI at *TMI*!"

"Sorry!" Tamara poured gracefully through the door, bag handles scooped over her wrists, tissues crumpled in both hands. Her nose looked raw at the tip and her eyes shot with red.

"Sorry I'm late! The kids are sick and the babysitter backed out, so I had to call Nasir at the last minute." She honked into a tissue and tossed it into the garbage can.

"Oh, totally insecure," Kevin was saying to the interviewer, leaning forward on the blue arm of the couch. He was wearing the same flannel shirt he'd had on when the police took him away the day before. "She spends every minute worrying about how she looks and what people think about her."

Despite the red nose Tamara looked completely put together, her hijab smooth and neat, makeup perfect, a camel coat draped stylishly over a loose silken blouse and trousers.

It was such a relief to see her that Beth wanted to cry. She rarely cried in her real life, but in this one, Regan Forrester's life, she seemed often on the edge of tears.

"If the kids are sick, you should be with them," Beth said, still on autopilot.

"They'll be fine." Tamara slung the bags onto the dining table. "I'm more worried about you." She followed as Beth wandered back into the bedroom, her face still glued to the video.

"Nah, I cut out because she's confused about her sexuality. Now she thinks she might be pansexual," Kevin was telling the interviewer, a sneer on his face. "She wants to explore or some shit."

"She's pan? Regan Forrester is pansexual?" The interviewer nearly hugged himself in joy. "OMG, that is breaking news!"

"Well, she sleeps with anything that moves," Kevin said. "Her manager. Her directors. Probably all of her co-stars. I mean, I felt like I had to keep an eye on her every second. Because, look at her, right? Who wouldn't want to hit that?"

"Um, not me personally, but I know what you mean, right?" the interviewer squealed.

Beth slumped into the chair beneath the window and Tamara gently withdrew the phone from her hand. "Sweetie. Don't look at it."

"I can't not." Beth took a shaky breath. In contrast to Tamara's stylishness, she was in the clothes she'd slept in, hair ratted, eyes sticky, face unwashed. "You've seen it?"

"I saw it last night, but that's when the youngest was puking everywhere, so I didn't get a chance to call you." Tamara sat on the bed—still unmade, which made Beth flinch—and took Beth's hands.

"Is it true?" Beth whispered. "About Mom drinking, and the . . ." She blinked up into Tamara's soft, concerned face. "Am I abusing prescription drugs?"

Tamara laughed lightly. "Sweetheart, I hope not. Have you talked to Eve?"

"No. I just saw the video now." Beth wanted to curl up in a ball. Apparently Regan and Eve had a deeper relationship than she guessed. She wondered if there was an anti-anxiety prescription in Regan's medicine cabinet somewhere, and if she should take one.

"I'll call Eve while you shower. She'll know what to do." Tamara tapped on the screen of the darkened phone.

"I had the idea that I might just crawl into bed, pull the covers over my head, and hide there all day eating ice cream and watching the Hallmark channel," Beth said. Since the apartment was already clean, that was her next line of response in a crisis.

"You can't. You have a day. There's the party tonight, for one thing. Satya Verinsky's birthday parties are legendary, and this one is on his boat. It will do you good to get out, be seen, have a little fun."

The thought of going out made Beth flinch again. In her real life, she loved a party, getting dressed up, meeting new people. Was this Regan Forrester's social anxiety? These feelings of nervousness, self-consciousness, and crowd avoidance were not Beth Barony at all. It was like Regan Forrester's reflexes were starting to influence Beth's mind.

The big good angel was taking over. What would happen to Beth's little good angel if it didn't get reseated in the right home?

"Eve and I made plans tonight," Beth said. "We can't cancel." It was more important than ever that she find Bene, reverse this spell, and get back into Beth Barony's body before Regan Forrester brought Beth's entire life crashing down around her ears.

Leaving Regan Forrester to mop up the spectacular mess Beth had made of Regan's. Guilt snaked through her gut along with the cold noodles.

"Plans?" Tamara raised a brow, waiting. But Beth didn't explain. She didn't know how much the other woman knew about the extremely unique situation Regan Forrester had gotten them into.

For that matter, she didn't know how much Eve knew. But Eve had recognized Bene's name when she said it. She seemed to understand the urgency.

Tamara's expression made Beth nervous. "Did you want to go to the party? We can do it after—Eve and I get our thing done." A promise that Regan would have to keep, since Beth would be out of here by end of day.

"Me? No, I'm not invited." Tamara forced another laugh. "You have got to stop treating me like I'm a movie star, like you. I'm a regular person."

I'm a regular person, Beth wanted to say. She'd miss Tamara, she realized. She liked the other woman's spunk and smarts. She was lovely.

So was Eve. Whom Regan had had an affair with, if Kevin was right.

Beth withdrew her hands. "I'm not sure how much of a movie star I'll be after everyone hears Kevin's interview," she said. "He seems to have dropped a few bombshells."

Tamara squeezed her fingers before letting go. "Eve will know what to do."

Eve was in the bedroom when Beth came out of the shower. The bed was made and Eve stood raking through Regan's closet, phone to her ear. From the front room came the open and shut of the refrigerator door, a click of dishes, Tamara on her own phone in a high-speed murmur. Eve's posture was tense but she looked like she'd just stepped off the cover of a magazine, her weave styled in big waves, makeup bold and gleaming. She too wore a pantsuit and the jacket hugged her bosom, the high waist showing off her curves and rear.

A burning thread snaked through Beth's belly. She'd felt this way when Timothy Kay kissed her. Arousal, and longing, raced along her nerves and lit up her nervous system.

Beth Barony wasn't attracted to women. But Regan Forrester was.

And Beth had Regan's stomach, her taste buds, her nervous system, and everything else.

Eve paused her conversation and assessed Beth, the wet hair, the plush purple towel, the bare feet. Her golden brown eyes flared, and Beth heated with embarrassment. Eve clicked off her phone and tucked it in her pocket, all business.

"All right, this day is about containing the damage from Shitstorm Kevin," she said. "You are scheduled for Ellen's show this morning, and we are going through with it. Then you have another interview for lunch. Everybody wants to talk to you right now, but I gave *Entertainment Weekly* the first chance. They'll call back if they want to do a cover shoot.

"Timothy scheduled filming this afternoon for that video you talked about, and then we'll make a reservation for dinner out somewhere before we go to Satya Verinsky's party. You are going to be seen. And you are not going to give a flying you-know-what about anything Kevin said about you."

"I have an item for the agenda," Beth said, moving to the second closet. "Bene."

"Who?" Tamara walked in the door, a glass of green liquid in her hand.

"One of Kevin's friends," Eve said without hesitation. "He sold Regan something, and she wants to give it back."

"What was it?" Tamara handed the glass to Beth.

Eve looked at her, eyebrows raised.

"An—ah—herbal remedy," Beth said. "It didn't work. I want my money back."

She sniffed the glass and wrinkled her nose. "Do I have to drink this?"

"Sorry, I thought this was your thing now. I notice there's been no fresh stuff since Saturday, though. Did no one make a delivery?"

"I don't know. I wasn't around yesterday afternoon."

"Performing missions of mercy." Eve swiped through hanger after hanger, scowling.

Beth pulled out a blouse and looked at it. "What video does Timothy want to shoot?"

"Ask him. I don't know anything about it." Eve shoved hangers with visible force. "Some public service announcement about staying in school. He said you talked about it last night. I was informed after the fact."

"That's right. We did talk about something like that."

Eve seemed angrier that Beth had made plans with Timothy than she had about Kevin's unauthorized interview. Beth picked out another blouse and compared them, trying to decide which one was less tarty. Both had plunging necklines and no sleeves. "This morning kind of put all that out of my mind."

"Want me to call about delivery?" Tamara asked. "The juice. Your diet, or whatever."

"Let's stop delivery," Beth said. "I'm going back to real food for a while." Regan might feel better in her body if she fed it proper nutrition.

Tamara's eyebrows rose. "That explain the noodles? They smell amazing."

"Finish them if you want," Beth said. "I'm not eating them."

She didn't think she could put anything in her belly this morning. Her stomach was jumping like a box full of frogs. Regan was going to teach Beth's class, Drew needed something and she didn't know what, and Kevin—the things he had said about Regan, the sneer on his face, the vitriol in his tone. Regan had slept with that man, shared her life with him, cared for him, possibly loved him. How could he turn on her with such venom? What was he so angry about?

She held the blouses up and looked at Eve. "Which one seems less trampy to you?"

Eve gave her the raised eyebrows again. Everyone was raising their eyebrows at her today. "We're worried about trampy now? That's new."

Beth clutched the clothes, shifting uncomfortably on her feet. "Eve—what he said about you and me. Kevin, I mean." She cleared her throat. "Did we—what I mean is . . . " She sucked in a breath. "What should I say?"

"Say whatever comes into your head." Eve strode out the door with magnificent grace, fury rippling off her. "You always do anyway."

She clamped her phone to her head and stepped into the hallway. The garbage bags still sat there, piled haphazardly, though it looked as if they'd been investigated by several sets of hands.

Tamara met Beth's eyes with an apologetic smile.

184 | MISTY URBAN

"She thinks you're going to take Kevin back. Like always."

"Not this time." Beth put one of the blouses back and pulled out the one set of trousers that Regan Forrester owned. She was going with the power suit, too. "Do you know who to call about picking up his stuff? Because otherwise I'm giving it to the Los Angeles Mission."

"I'll call the Mission." Tamara hovered in the doorway.

Beth cleared her throat again, glancing beyond her, looking for Eve. "Is she mad because—it's out in the open now?"

Tamara shrugged and picked a hairbrush off the dressing table. "Eve doesn't care who knows about her affairs. But she knows you'll have to deny it."

"Will I? Really?"

That seemed cruel. Except that everyone who wanted to know what Regan Forrester ate for lunch would also love to know who she slept with. It grabbed headlines when any celebrity admitted to a non-straight orientation. Regan Forrester admitting she could be attracted to all sorts of genders would snag global attention.

Beth held still while Tamara drew the brush through her waves of wet hair and wrapped it up in a quick chignon. She'd known that tossing Kevin out under police escort could hurt Regan's image and tank her career. She'd done it anyway. While Regan was determined to swoop in and save Beth's class.

The guilt bit again, and Beth shook it off. Regan Forrester's problems with her ex-lovers were not

Beth's problems. Beth's problems were that Regan Forrester had dug into her life and didn't seem to want to let go. It made her want to scream, and spit nails, and tear something with her bare hands.

It made her worry less about protecting Regan and preserving her life. It made her care less about the state the girl found herself in once Bene managed to yank her back into her own body. Beth would have her own damage control to do, repairing her relationships, rescuing her class, making sure her loved ones didn't think she'd gone completely mad. She felt mad. She wanted to wreck something. She wanted to burn something down to the ground and see what came writhing out of the ashes.

She was so angry she trembled with it. This wasn't like her, either. She was losing herself. Losing Beth Barony. She *had* to get her back.

Dressed in blouse and slacks and a pair of strappy black sandals with cushioned soles, with minimal makeup since she'd get it done at the show, Beth grabbed her purse and stepped out the door with the two women flanking her. She had to talk to Eve about when they could go see Bene, but Eve was busy doing an Internet search, finding out how many entertainment sites had already picked up Kevin McDonald's late-night interview rants and his shocking accusations about his ex.

"I need something to put on your social media accounts," Tamara said in a worried tone. "We have to come out with some positive PR in the face of this."

"Everyone's going to want to see what Regan

Forrester does in response." Not looking up from her phone, Eve stabbed one ruby-tipped fingernail in the button for the ground floor.

"I've got a platform, have I?"

Beth clamped the strap of her purse over her chest as if it might offer protection. There was no more thinking about what Regan Forrester would want or do. She was clinging to Beth Barony as hard as she could before she slipped away.

"Then I want to publish three messages today. First, I want you to post the number of the National Domestic Violence Hotline."

Eve lifted her eyes from her phone. Tamara's mouth dropped open.

"Later," Beth said, "I want you to post a list of the shelters available in Los Angeles for women experiencing domestic violence or homelessness. And tonight, I want you to post statistics on violence against women. Not just the crimes but the cost of it. Health costs, sick days, the productivity women lose due to assault and harassment. The number of women who are killed by domestic homicides each year. The numbers should be on a website somewhere, and if they're not, Jo—I can get them for you." Joan would be so proud of her. "And maybe post a link to something about the Violence Against Women Act while you're at it."

"You're going to lose followers," Eve warned. "People don't like it when celebrities go activist."

Tamara looked back and forth between them. "Everyone's going to assume it's an accusation against Kevin."

"I'm not making any accusations."

Beth curled her fingers around the strap. Dressing like Beth Barony would when she was teaching or attending a professional conference made her feel more like herself, centered, confident. The person she was. The person she wanted to go back to.

"I'm not turning this into a he-said-she-said scenario. I'm not hiding in shame. I'm sharing information that will save women's lives."

She stepped out the apartment door into what looked like a crowd of protesters. Except they weren't protesters. They were a group of people armed with cameras and cell phones, all waiting for Regan Forrester.

"Regan! Is it true you broke up with Kevin McDonald? Have you seen the interview he gave yesterday for *Celebrity TMI*?"

"Is it true you're pansexual?"

"Is it true you had an affair with your manager? Ms. Adesina, do you care to comment on that?"

"I do not," Eve said coolly. She stood close to Beth's shoulder. Tamara, foiled by the press of bodies as she tried to move away, hovered at Beth's other side, looking nervous.

"Is it true you called the cops on Kevin McDonald?"

"Is it true you cheated on him several times during your relationship?"

"Don't say anything," Eve muttered in her ear. "Just push on through."

Beth knew she was right and tried to do just that.

But the next question touched a nerve.

"Is it true your mother is an alcoholic?"

"It's not fair to bring Mom into it," she murmured to Eve.

"We're all in it," Eve said, jaw set in tight lines. She held out one arm like a bodyguard, guiding Beth toward the black car parked at the curb. Beth's stomach flip-flopped. She hoped she wasn't going to throw up on the street.

"Come on, Regan! Talk to us! We want to know. Is it true you're addicted to prescription drugs? Was that why the police were called to your building yesterday?"

Beth snapped. She whirled around and stared at the man asking the question. "I am not addicted to prescription drugs." Recalling the jumble of orange cannister in Regan's medicine cabinet, all with the directions to take "as needed," Beth really hoped that was true. If only Regan had checked for Beth's birth control pills before she started sleeping with her husband morning, noon, and night.

"And yes, the police did come to my building. Want to know why?" The cell phones sprouted before her face. Eve's fingers curled around her arm, but the snarling creature that had coiled in Beth's belly all morning sprang to the surface.

"There was a domestic violence incident in my building this weekend. A man shouting at his girlfriend, threatening to kill her. She was afraid for her life. She was afraid he had a gun. But someone called the police for her, and they arrived before she was hurt, and her boyfriend got an intervention and hopefully the help he needs. Not everybody would make that call. A lot of people would just close their doors and say it's none of their business."

Beth looked at each of the suddenly quiet faces, into the cameras clicking steadily. Eve tugged at her arm. Beth followed, but craned her neck to face the crowd.

"I want to thank whoever it was who called the police and was brave enough to call for help when they thought someone else was in trouble. I hope all you will make that call when you see someone getting harassed or hurt."

The rising lump in her throat cut off her tirade. Instead she gave them Beth Barony's Teacher Look, the one that froze fractious or complaining students in their seats. "Anything else?"

A slim young woman with a severe black bob and thick black eyebrows raised her hand. "Yes?" Beth said.

"Koko Koyama for *Star News*," the reporter said sweetly. "The pansexual thing?"

Beth gulped. It was not her place to out Regan Forrester. No matter how angry she was at the girl right this moment.

"I am not confused about my sexuality," Beth said instead. "I understand my sexuality very well, and I don't feel like discussing it with anyone." She pointed at the young woman. "But pansexual does not mean promiscuous, as Kevin McDonald implied. Put that in the quote, please."

She let Eve and Tamara stuff her into the car. Beth lifted her chin as Eve pinned her with a look.

"Happy now?" Eve snapped. "That's going to be everywhere. All of it."

Beth's chest felt like she was tearing in half. Her lungs hurt, and the noodles in her stomach writhed like snakes. She felt vengeful, rageful, charged with power. Tearing things open and exposing the truth gave her a rush. She wanted to keep tearing, crushing, chewing up lies and spitting them out until everything was stripped down to bare, awful reality.

She wasn't being fair. She couldn't crater Regan Forrester's life and then step out of it as easily as a snake shedding its skin. Could she?

She stared back at Eve, her gaze hard. "When's our date with Bene?"

Eve's eyes fell to her phone. "Seven o'clock."

"Then ask me again if I'm happy at, oh, seven fifteen."

Beth sat back in her seat, staring out the window through the tinted glass. All of the people she was looking at had busy inner lives, aspirations, dreams. Many of them likely had some problem that seemed crushing or insurmountable. No doubt a number of them had something going on in their life that had spun them completely off their axis.

Regan Forrester, it seemed, had been keeping a tight lid on any number of secrets. So tight a lid that the pressure of them popped her out of her own life and into Beth's.

How strange life was, Beth thought darkly. How indescribable in its essence, unknowable in its core. The things she would have said three days ago were her essential, knowable self had all been cast into doubt and disarray. She was sure of nothing anymore. The world was suddenly larger, more complex, more dangerous than anything Beth Barony had ever encountered in her safe, Midwestern, middle-class life.

The revelation was terrifying and awe-inspiring. She wanted to talk about it with someone, but the only person in the world who could possibly understand was standing before the summer honors lit class in Eden Prairie's International School, destroying every bit of Beth's credibility as a teacher.

Tamara and Eve sat with her in a fraught, pensive silence. She was putting their careers at risk, too.

"Look," Beth said gently. "I know I've been off my rocker this weekend. I've been under some . . . stress."

Tamara nodded with understanding, her brown eyes large and soft. Eve snorted.

"Girl, you been a mess since you got back with Kevin the last time." Eve's big, dark eyes with their impossible lashes swept Beth from head to toe, and for a moment she felt like the other woman saw inside her. "We want you back," she said softly.

"You'll get me. Her. The real Regan," Beth said. "She'll be back tomorrow. I promise. Bear with me one more day, please?"

Eve exchanged a look with Tamara. "You ever met the *real* Regan?"

"Not sure that I have, honestly," Tamara replied.

"You'll love her," Beth said. Panic squeezed her upper chest. She felt dizzy, light-headed, like the top of her head was floating away. "She's really great."

She was surprised to realize it. She cared for Regan Forrester, that headstrong, wily, vulnerable girl. She wanted to nurture and protect her. She also wanted to slap her out of Beth's life back into her own.

"We can cancel today," Tamara said. "Take it easy. It's going to be like this everywhere you go."

"And miss being on The Ellen DeGeneres Show?" Beth said. "You can't keep me away. My—" She'd almost said daughter. She had a daughter? She groped in her mind for the girl's name. *Abby. Pull yourself together, Beth!* Her name was Beth Barony. She was married to a wonderful man. She had two children, Abby and Drew. She was an English teacher, debate team coach, and a mom.

She could not let Regan Forrester erase her. Not even for the chance of being on The Ellen DeGeneres Show. "We can't meet with Bene any earlier?" she asked Eve.

"No." The other woman slipped her phone back in her pocket and regarded Beth with an even stare. "Since everything else is on the table today, you want to talk about us?"

Beth closed her eyes and breathed through her nose the way she did at the doctor's when she had to get blood drawn. "Ask me tomorrow," she said. "We can talk tomorrow. Just help me get through today."

18 · THE FILM

"So. One of Regan Forrester's causes is getting kids to stay in school."

Timothy Kay was leaning against the wall outside her dressing room when Beth emerged. A warm tingle rushed down her spine.

She'd spent the last three hours with him, filming a funny skit with a message about encouraging kids to finish high school and explore their options after. She'd said something in passing, the night before, when he talked about a friend who was producing a series of skits with big-name actors giving public service messages. Rather flippantly she'd given him a list of Beth Barony's causes. Overnight he had booked time at the studio and come up with a script for Regan Forrester to cajole local kids to graduate high school.

A stunt to promote his movie, no more. Not an excuse to spend time with her. But it had proved a wonderful three hours. She enjoyed the time spent with him, laughing, talking, trying new takes on a scene. Since she was acting like a teacher, her natural role, the camera hadn't made her feel uncomfortable at all. She was dressed in normal clothes, made up no more than a normal person, saying lines Beth Barony would say before teenagers who acted a great deal like Beth Barony's students. She'd forgotten, for a while, that she was wearing Regan Forrester's face.

Maybe she was getting good at this. Maybe she

could be an actress after all. Maybe she, Beth Barony, could do more with Regan Forrester's gifts than Regan herself had.

Beth froze. What an awful, betraying, hideously arrogant thought. What was *happening* to her?

"This is a cause dear to my heart," Beth said, feeling shy. Timothy fell into step with her as they headed down the narrow hallway of the studio to the front doors. She didn't see Eve or Tamara anywhere, though the place was full of people.

"You spoke really well about college."

"Best years of my life," Beth said, then bit her lip.

She kept forgetting around him that she was supposed to be Regan Forrester. Until his dark eyes ran over every inch of her and she remembered he was looking at Regan Forrester's perfect body, clad in a demure pantsuit.

"I mean, that's what everyone says, right? But of course I never went to college. I got my GED while I was working on a soap opera. Which you probably know."

"And where, I understand, you met Kevin McDonald. Who seems to be really, really angry with you right now."

Timothy held a door open for her, and Beth felt the heat of his body as she moved past. His scent drifted through her nose to the top of her head.

It wasn't cologne. It was soap, Irish Spring. The soap Barony used. Maybe that was why the scent of Timothy Kay made her want to curl up against his chest and wrap her arms and legs around him. He reminded her of her husband.

"That's over," Beth said. "Done. He's not happy about it."

"So I gathered." He held open the outer door to the street, touching the small of her back as she walked through. The gesture was unnecessary, and very slight, but it felt protective. "I heard Ellen brought up the emergency protective order."

"The show hasn't aired yet," Beth said dryly, waiting while other people took advantage of the door he held and shoved through.

"I got a call," he explained, joining her on the sidewalk.

Beth slid on her sunglasses and looked around, blinking. The world looked so bright, so normal. Disorienting after spending hours before a camera in artificial light. She wasn't sure she'd ever get used to the bright California sunshine. It seemed clearer, sharper than Minnesota sunshine. The sky was a paler blue, as if washed out by the heat, and it made everything look more dramatic. Staged.

What was she thinking? She didn't have to get used to this. She had to get back to her Minnesota summer, her cerulean Minnesota sky, her Minnesota everything, very soon.

"You *do* keep tabs on things," she said.

"Or maybe just you." He slid on his own glasses so she couldn't decipher his expression. "Want to get a bite to eat? I know a place a couple of blocks from here. Small, not too pretentious. No press."

"My favorite kind of place."

Eve had said she'd make reservations somewhere Regan could be seen. But Beth didn't want to be seen. She wanted to be quiet and invisible. She wanted to be herself again.

Besides, she wasn't sure she could keep anything down. After an hour in the chair getting her hair blown out and makeup troweled on, fifteen minutes before a live studio audience being grilled by Ellen on every dramatic reveal Kevin McDonald had made in his late-night rant, a lunch of being further filleted by a reporter who couldn't be much older than Drew, and then the taping with Timothy, she felt burnt to the socket. Her body felt like she was coming apart at the seams.

"I'm meeting Eve at seven for—an appointment," she remembered. "I assume she can pick me up."

"Or I can take you."

He strolled easily beside her, hands in his pockets. People on the sidewalk didn't jostle her with Timothy Kay at her side. They stared, and held up their cell phones to take a picture, but nobody stopped or followed them. She almost felt like a normal person again.

"No, it's something we need to do."

"So I assume Ellen wanted to know all about your affair with Eve."

Beth's stomach swam around under her skin. The sun jabbed like sharp needles. "At least Ellen wasn't judgmental about it. She clearly could understand why Re—why I might be attracted."

"And that's what broke you and Kevin up last time?"

At the crosswalk he angled his body between her and the street, as if shielding her from oncoming cars. Beth had never had a man be chivalrous to her before. Barony was the best of men but he assumed she could take care of herself. It was sweet to have someone else look after her.

"No, Eve and I—happened after Kevin and I broke up." She'd learned that much from Tamara. "But when we got back together, he held it over me. Over both of us, I think," Beth guessed.

"I imagine he felt threatened. If he thought you were—what's the word? Pan."

"I'm not sure he understands what it means," Beth said, her lip curling. "He used it to suggest I sleep with everything that comes along."

Timothy's face turned her way. He put out an arm to shield her as a woman trundled by, laden down with bags bearing designer labels. "I'm not sure I understand what it means," he admitted.

Beth thought of her students and the tender revelations they made in their reading journals, the occasional tear-filled session in her office, the talks she'd had as Sherice's daughter, Blessing, tried to educate her on what the world was like for them. She hadn't really understood, hadn't been able to see beyond her own worldview. Until now.

But she couldn't talk about her students with Timothy Kay. He was looking at Regan Forrester's face.

Regan might have a real chance with him, when she came back. A pang of regret snuck beneath her ribs. Beth would miss his attention. She liked the way they were together. She enjoyed the flare of attraction, desiring and feeling desired, even though it was dangerous and morally questionable and a betrayal of her wedding vows.

How had Blessing put it? "Pan means you can feel attracted to people of any gender or sexuality," Beth explained as they crossed another street. The way she felt attracted to Timothy Kay, towering above her, his chest expansively broad as he held open the door of the restaurant so she could pass. The lust dived and splashed with the other feelings roiling in her belly.

"But that doesn't mean you necessarily act on every attraction." Beth folded her sunglasses and put them in her bag. "That's what Kevin never got. I'm actually not promiscuous at all. It's hard for me to be intimate with people. I have to have an emotional connection first."

The words echoed oddly in her head as she said them. She was speaking for herself, Beth Barony, and yet the confession had the resonance of truth in Regan Forrester's body. Beth's head pounded. It was getting harder to think of herself as separate. As Beth.

"That's good to know." Timothy came to stand beside her in the small waiting area of the restaurant. Close beside her.

"Are you threatened?" she asked boldly, glancing up at his face.

"Only because it increases the competition." He folded his own sunglasses and slipped them in a pocket as a server approached.

Beth turned to follow the server, heat weaving over her neck. It was the closest he'd come to an admission. Well, that and their endless, all-consuming, delirium-inducing marathon of kissing—that had been an admission of sorts. She wanted a chance to explore this.

No, she didn't. The only thing she wanted to explore was the mojo that would put her back into Beth Barony's body. Beth Barony's squishy, scarred, nearing middle age and close to menopausal body.

Do you really want to give up all this?

Yes, Beth screamed back to the voice in her head. She wanted to give up this lithe, firm, gloriously perfect twenty-four year-old body and this equally flawless, internationally recognized face. Give up the chance to live the prime decades of her life being a rich, beautiful actress living in one of the most interesting cities in the world.

Although when she put it that way . . .

"I gather your mom won't like what he said about her," Timothy said as they reached their table.

"That she's abusing alcohol and refuses to get treatment? It's no more than I've said to her, several times."

Beth dropped into a chair and spread the napkin over her lap. "She stops talking to me every time I bring it up, and then claims I'm holding some grudge against her." She wondered where these words were coming from. They felt automatic. Like she was accessing Regan Forrester's memories, Regan Forrester's past.

That couldn't be possible. Regan Forrester's past, her memories, her consciousness, her little good angel, all of them were currently in Minnesota, inside Beth's big good angel. Was Regan Forrester starting to access Beth's memories? Did Regan feel like Beth's body was starting to come apart?

Or did she feel like the charade was becoming more real? That it was becoming easier and easier to inhabit Beth, to *be* Beth? Was that why she didn't want to come back?

She picked up a menu so she had something to do with her hands. There was no possible way she could eat anything.

"I think the biggest surprise," Timothy observed as he settled into his chair, "was that your dad was Haitian. I don't think anyone knew that."

She shot a glance over the table while their server brought glasses of water with ice. "Regan Forrester is half Black? Does that change anything?"

He raised a cool eyebrow at her challenge. "It just seems curious that it never came up before."

Beth hid behind her menu. Her hands shook slightly. How would Regan feel about these revelations? When Ellen asked about her childhood in Alabama, Beth told her about hiding in the bathroom during lunch in middle school to avoid teasing. When she said the words it felt not as if she were sharing a story Regan Forrester had told her but reliving something she had herself experienced, a traumatic memory burned into her body, into her cells.

It wasn't just guilt making her chest hurt so fiercely. She'd all but publicly labeled her boyfriend an abuser. She'd made Regan's past, her mother's past, her father's past a matter of public record as well. Oh, and if Ellen was right, she was the new poster child for pansexuality.

Whatever good Beth had tried to do in Regan's life—protect her female friendships, encourage kids to stay in school—she still got to go back to her safe, quiet life in her safe, quiet town, while Regan had to come back here to face the consequences of what Kevin McDonald had brought to light, because of Beth. Not all her beauty, fame, youth, and Hollywood glamour could protect her from a man who was determined to bring her down.

And Beth was mad because Regan had slept with Beth's husband? There was just no comparison.

Maybe she shouldn't see Bene yet. Maybe she owed it to Regan to stay here and face the firestorm. How could she yank Regan back into her world when Beth had turned it into a minefield?

She had fooled Regan and Tamara so far. She had even fooled Regan's mom. Timothy seemed like he would protect her, and she had a contract for his next movie. She could hire an acting coach and take classes. It was kind of fun to dress up in expensive gowns and parade around being photographed. Satya Verinsky's party sounded like it was one of the celebrity events of the year, something she'd always remember. She wouldn't mind a couple more days with Timothy.

And there was something a bit daring about it, even sitting here in this restaurant, realizing when people recognized her and Timothy and tried to take discreet photos. She wasn't just an average celebrity now; after Kevin's performance, she was a trending hashtag. There was something heady about that kind of power, though it wasn't hers and it wasn't earned and it was entirely undeserved.

Beth put a hand to her chest as she felt something tearing, deep and possibly final. How could she even *think* these things? Was she actually considering staying in Regan's life?

Just until Wednesday, a small voice in her head argued. Then she could go back to the Vodou temple she'd found, ask the priest and priestess, the *hougan* and the *manbo*, to put her little good angel back where she belonged. It would only be a few more days. Didn't she owe it to Regan to try?

Her phone buzzed from its place above her plate, where she had put it out of habit, the habit of a mother who was available every second to her kids. The display showed Beth's cell phone number. The text message read *You won't believe what we did!* And the picture showed a woman's forearm with a tiny circle and small lines waving from it, a black sun outlined in the angry red of a fresh tattoo.

A primal terror, deep and unreasoning, swamped Beth's every sense. She nearly fainted. "Excuse me," she muttered, snatching the phone to her chest. "I need to make a call." She was dialing before she was out the door.

19 · THE TATTOO

"**C**alm down! Beth! Calm down!" Regan laughed. Regan Forrester was laughing at her.

Beth stood on a sidewalk in the middle of Los Angeles, city dwellers and tourists staring at her curiously while she hyperventilated, and Regan Forrester laughed.

"It's Joan's tattoo. She's celebrating. The thousandth woman to be successfully placed out of the shelter during her time as director."

Beth clutched the phone with both hands. The sun pounded down on her face, hurting her eyes. Her chest felt pulled in every compass point. Even her feet hurt, as if the pavement were melting the thick soles of her sandals.

"I should be there," Beth wailed. "I told Joan I'd go with her to get her tattoo. She's talked about it for years."

"I told her I'd get one to match." Regan laughed again. "Except, Beth! You are deathly afraid of needles! I thought I was going to pass out just stepping into the shop. What is your deal?"

"I don't know."

The breath heaved out of her throat, coarse and narrow in her upper chest. So Regan was picking up on Beth's body's traumas, just as Beth was absorbing Regan's. "I hate needles. When I was a kid I had to get a series of rabies shots when we thought I'd been bitten by a bat, and needles have freaked me out ever since."

"Huh. Maybe that's it. I've been totally creeped out since the minute we got here and I have, like, five tattoos. But I promised Joanie."

Five? Beth had only seen two of them, one on the wrist and one on an ankle. She wondered where the others were placed.

"*I* promised Joan," Beth muttered. "Me. I'm Joanie's best friend. *I* am."

"Well, I'm standing in for you today, hon, and you're lucky I did. You would have fainted the minute you walked through the door."

That was very likely true. The sick swirl in Beth's stomach thickened. "How was class?"

"Class! Oh my gosh, you won't believe this."

The swirl sank. Beth put a hand to her forehead and looked around for a place to sit. "Oh, no. How bad was it?"

"Bad?" Again that laugh. It didn't sound like Beth's laugh, not the laugh she heard in her head. "It was amazing! I had no idea teaching was so fun!"

"They liked the movie?" Beth felt the sidewalk sway beneath her feet. Was she experiencing an earthquake? People pushed past her, heads turning as they recognized Regan Forrester. She didn't have the energy to care. "I'm glad, I guess."

"Oh, no, we didn't do the movie. We just talked about the book. I had them act out different scenes from the novel so we could discuss character motivations and all that other stuff in your notes. They were a little quiet and shy at first, but once they got going, holy cow. The things they came up with!"

"Like what?" Beth asked, her stomach shifting. It didn't sound like her class had been a disaster that Beth needed to come home and fix.

"Oh, I asked them to tell me the goals and backstory for their characters, and I taught them method acting, and it was just so amazing, the energy in the room! They had this incredible discussion about character motivations. Then I asked them your questions in the margins, like whether Heathcliff is half Black and has all this internalized racism because of colonialism and stuff, and is Cathy rebelling against society's rules about women and whatever, and wow, it was so intense! Some of them asked if they could do their final project on how Brontë is critiquing the prejudices in her society about rural people and mixed races and expectations on women."

Regan sounded giddy. "I loved it. They really got it. *I* really got it. I think if I didn't want to be a fashion designer, I would want to be a teacher."

Beth swallowed against the hot, hard lump in her throat. "I thought you wanted to be an actor."

"Good thing I am!" Regan said brightly. "That's why things went okay today. But I always wanted to design clothes, ever since I was little. I thought modeling would help me learn how to do that, which is why I went along with Mom. And then she moved us to LA and I kept getting cast in things, and it seemed like a good way to make money."

Beth's head whirled. Things went okay? It sounded like Regan had transformed her class. They'd been bumps on a log for Beth, but for Regan, they'd come alive. They were already thinking about their final projects. Beth put a hand on her chest. Was this heartburn? Food poisoning? Had there been something off about that pad Thai?

"What about the meeting with Dean Chavez?"

"Pushed back. She was busy, so we'll do it later. And, oh! I talked to Drew."

Beth staggered into a lamp post and leaned against it. "Did something happen? Is he all right?"

"Just really nervous about the final competition. He's going up against the top athletes in the country in his events, Beth! Did you know that?"

No, Beth thought, she didn't. She hadn't known because she was stuck in someone else's body and she couldn't call her kids using someone else's voice, and therefore she had no idea what was going on with them. Meanwhile, they were calling Regan Forrester for advice.

"What did you tell him?"

"Just that all the best athletes use visualization to help improve their performance. I taught him some of the techniques that my therapist taught me to do."

Beth felt like an axe had come down from the heavens, cleaving her in two. Regan Forrester had won over Beth's husband, her friends, her neighbor, her literature class, and now she had won over her kids.

Everybody in her life was going to be disappointed when the real Beth Barony came back.

"Regan." Beth forced herself to breathe. "I am so grateful for that. For everything. You have been so good about this entire weird and unbelievable venture." She gave a shaky laugh. "I think you're better at my life than I am." While Beth Barony had done nothing, nothing to improve Regan Forrester's lot. "But I'm going to see Bene tonight, and he's going to switch us back."

A long silence met her from the other end of the call. "Regan?"

"I was kind of hoping to have one more night." The voice on the other end was soft, subdued. "Sit in the hot tub. Drink some wine. Read a book." Another long pause. "Do you know the last time I read a book? I *like* reading now."

Beth gripped the phone, willing herself to remain calm. She'd ended up here, how she didn't know, because Regan Forrester wanted to escape her life. And now Beth was yanking her back to it, after making a series of changes that Regan hadn't asked for and would likely not approve.

"I'm sorry," Beth said lamely. "But Regan, you have so much here. You have such terrific people around you. I love Tamara. And Eve—she's amazing. She's beyond words."

Regan's laugh was small and tremulous. "That's for sure."

"I know I ruined things with Kevin," Beth went on. "But he is bad, bad, bad for you. And Timothy Kay likes you."

"Timothy Kay?"

"Likes you," Beth confirmed. "A lot." She glanced inside the restaurant and saw Timothy unfolding his long form from the table, chatting with another patron, probably a fan. "I'm getting the sense that his sequel might actually be a good movie, if he gets to go with his own creative choices. And you'll get lots of offers for good roles, I'm sure. Ellen loved you today."

"Ellen loved *you*," Regan said quietly. In her voice was a thread of warning.

Beth drew a deep breath. "Regan, it's your life. You get to live it. Don't you want this incredible body? This face? Do you even understand how lucky you are?" She tried to bring her voice to a non-shouting level. "You have so many choices, so many opportunities. No matter how awful or hopeless things might seem right now, you can always choose something else."

"What if I have chosen?" The voice on the other end, as if answering Beth's anger, gained in strength. "What if I don't want to be important or famous or an influencer or a leader or a role model or any of that shit? What if I just want to be a person? What if I want a husband, and kids, and a real job, and real friends, and a boring normal life? I could even have a real dad."

Her laugh was short, bitter. "He called me today. Your dad. I'm in love. He said he started a chess group and is singing in a barbershop quartet at his senior living place, and they're having a swing dance on Saturday. He asked me to be his date." Her voice shook with tears. "I always wanted a dad."

Beth felt like crying, too, but she could not be Regan Forrester having a breakdown on a public sidewalk in Los Angeles, not outside a trendy restaurant where most of the people walking past her know who she was. Or thought they knew.

"I'm sorry, Regan. But that's *my* boring, normal life," she choked. "I built it. I chose it. I want it back."

"No, you don't." The words flew at her like a slap. "You wanted out. That's the only way the spell would work. I had to find someone who would switch places with me. Do you know how many times I tried that spell? How much it cost me? I was almost ready to give up, I was so close to crazy, and Kevin—" The sobs were audible, and real. "You wanted out, Beth. You wanted the trade. You don't get to back out now because you got the bum side of the deal."

"I never wanted to leave my life," Beth whispered. She heard the words over the buzzsaw growling in her head. Her temples throbbed like her skull might crack open. "I just wondered what other lives might feel like. Yours, as it happened. But I never wanted *out*."

"I won't do it," Regan said. "I won't agree. You think I want to come back and work at a soup kitchen and go on shows and talk about how interesting I am? I don't want the whole world to discuss my sexuality, Beth! It's nobody else's business. And I never wanted to be a Black actor. I just wanted to be an actor, period. But I don't have that option anymore."

"I'm sorry," Beth whispered. "But isn't it a relief to be able to say the truth?"

"Oh, yeah." Regan's laugh had turned bitter. "Honesty gets you so much in this business. You don't have any idea what it's like, Beth. You can't."

She didn't. She knew that. She'd had barely a glimpse into the kinds of pressure her career put on Regan. She had to watch everything she said, everything she wore. She had to be sexy and appealing and the center of attention but also be hirable and a bankable star.

She had to go to shoots and interviews and offer herself up endlessly as a subject of discussion and judgment. She had to conform to the most unreal standards of beauty and yet make her beauty appear natural and effortless. And whatever was hurting her, she couldn't talk about, because it was immediately turned into a cause.

No wonder Regan wanted Beth's blissfully anonymous life.

Beth rubbed her forehead as Regan's words pounded through it. "How much of this is Joan overhearing?" she asked.

"I went out to the car," Regan snapped. "The Volvo. Your Volvo. And you know what else? I love this car. I love driving it. I feel like a mom in this car. I feel like a wife. I'm pretty sure I could feel like a teacher. I'm a damn good actress, you know."

"You're a terrific actress." Beth's voice was a whimper, a plea. It was true. Beth would never, ever have guessed from her movies, from her interviews, from all the shots of her on the red carpet, what was really going on in Regan Forrester's head. How much she wanted something else for her life. Just like Beth had.

"Regan, I will help you, I'll do whatever I can—"

"You've already helped me," Regan cut her off. "You've given me a skin I don't want to climb out of every second. I like it here. I'm staying."

"Then what happens to me?" Beth could barely hear over the storm in her head, reverberating in her chest. "What happens with the spell if you won't switch back?"

"I don't know, and I don't care. You can stay Regan Forrester. Good luck with that."

Beth clung to the lamp post while the sidewalk tilted and her stomach heaved. "Are you feeling this?" she whispered. "Like you're coming apart at the seams? I don't think we have a choice, Regan."

"Call me Beth," Beth's voice said to her. "I like that name. Beth. Bethie. Maybe Betty when I'm in the mood. Know what? I don't think I'm scared of needles anymore. I'm going to get a tattoo with my best friend Joan, and then we're going out for dinner, and then I have a class to plan for tomorrow."

Beth caught the slam of a car door, the determined stamp of feet, the jingle of a shop door opening, and then the sound of her voice projecting loudly enough for Joan and the rest of the shop to hear.

"Goodbye, Regan. I don't think you should call me again. Good luck with your life."

The call disappeared. Beth sucked in huge gasps of air. Dizzy, she bent over, groping for her knees. She wondered what was going to give out first—her head, her legs, her stomach. A strong arm slipped around her, hard, firm, warm.

"Bad news?" Timothy said, drawing her up.

Beth sagged against him in relief. He was so solid, he felt so real, and he smelled so good, so normal and safe, that she nearly wept.

Regan wasn't coming apart like she was.

Regan meant to stay in her body, in her life.

What happened if Beth's soul, her consciousness, tore out of Regan's body like an alien birth? Where would she go? What would happen to her? Would she even continue to exist?

"I need—Eve," she gasped. "Right now."

"All right. Let's call her."

He sounded so normal. So sane, in a world where nothing made sense.

Beth tipped up her chin and stared at him. "I'm going to miss you," she said.

"Hey." His hand slid into her hair, cupping the back of her head. "Aren't you coming to Satya's party tonight? I'll see you there."

"I don't know if I'll make it." Her voice shook. It wasn't *her* voice. This wasn't her body, these weren't her clothes, and this man looking with gentle concern into her eyes wasn't hers, either. He might have been, if she'd made a different choice. Still yet could make it.

His scent wafted past her, clean, sharp, arousing. Irish Spring. *Barony.*

"If I don't see you—I just want you to know—I've had a really good time."

She couldn't mean that. She'd been miserable every minute of these past three days. Hadn't she?

No, whispered that voice of honesty in her head.

She hadn't.

"I hope there are more good times," Timothy Kay said, wrapping another strong arm around her and pulling her close.

Beth closed her eyes and sank into his kiss, savoring it as long as she could. There wouldn't be more good times, not for them. And maybe not for her, ever.

She let the prince kiss her, long, slow, and thorough. She felt the thrill to her toes, mixed with regret over what might have been.

And now she needed to go wake herself up.

20 • THE PERISTYLE

"So," Beth said once she and Eve were in the long black car, shielded behind the tinted windows, and the driver set off for the destination Eve had given him. "Where did you say Bene lives?"

Eve turned from the window. "You don't look right."

"I don't feel right," Beth confessed. "I'm hoping he'll fix that."

Eve lifted one elegant shoulder. She was still wearing the pant suit, but the top of her blouse was unbuttoned, showing deep cleavage and the top of a lacy lavender bra.

"I can't believe I went back to Kevin after you," Beth blurted.

Dusk was falling into the LA canyons, the sun slipping away behind the Hollywood sign Beth still hadn't seen. The back of the hired car felt safe and intimate, the time for confessions.

Too bad Beth felt like she was being quartered, the punishment for traitors in the old days, when horses pulled a person in four directions and the remains were hung up as a warning to others.

"I figured he threatened you somehow, to make you take him back. Telling on us, I suppose." Eve glanced at her phone, her thumb moving over the screen.

"How did we meet Bene?" Beth asked.

Eve looked up with an odd expression. "You'll

have to ask Kevin that."

"Oh. Somehow I thought you knew him."

"I introduced you to Vodou," Eve said with a note of irritation in her satiny voice. "You're the one who went off script."

"That's right," Beth said. "I gather the *bokor* types aren't really condoned."

She wondered what Eve wanted of Regan, or Regan of Eve. That was something else Regan would have to sort out. Beth's problem was that she felt like someone had carved away the top of her head and left her brain exposed, quivering in the cold air. Flashes of heat darted through her nervous system, fleeing down her spine and shooting everywhere. It took her mind off her throbbing head and queasy stomach.

"I suppose I was—um—trying to find out something about my dad. My Haitian heritage?" She winced as Eve gave her a scornful look. "I honestly don't remember."

"I think Kevin was up to something," Eve said, "but I doubt you'd tell me what it was."

For a wild second Beth wanted to confess everything. Eve seemed like the one person in Regan's life who would listen to a wildly far-fetched, improbable tale of body swapping and not immediately turn her over for psychiatric evaluation.

And maybe Timothy. And possibly her mother as well. For as much as she judged and belittled, Beth sensed there was real affection behind Mrs. Forrester's concern.

And even if she did think Regan was off her rocker, Tamara would lend a listening ear and probably offer to run get food. Regan did have people in her life who cared deeply for her. She didn't really want to leave them behind?

But Regan would be loved wherever she went, and now she knew that. The little wretch had stolen the affections of Beth's husband, children, students, and cat. And now she was stealing Beth's car, her dream car, the one she'd saved up for, and vowing to get a tattoo. Enough was enough.

"I don't think any of us want to know what Kevin was up to," Beth said, and prepared herself to meet Bene.

They turned onto a street lined with shops, not high-end boutiques but a mix of businesses that felt like behind-the-scenes LA. The car stopped before one that seemed a cross between a pharmacy and a new age store. Hemp products hung in the window above a plush counter scattered with candles, charms, and gemstones. The air, when Eve led her inside, smelled of incense and ash. The sharp odor burrowed into Beth's head.

Musical instruments hung from the walls, all sorts of drums and rattles, with neat rows of marijuana pipes in various sizes below. Racks of clothing crowded the floor space, leaving barely enough room to squeeze through.

Beth banged her knee against a shelf of books and looked down. The shelves were piled with books about Wicca, lucid dreaming, astral projection, and the medicinal uses of LSD.

"Can I help you," a clerk intoned, coming out from behind a counter painted bright blue.

The clerk wore a suit jacket and men's tie paired with a pleated school uniform skirt, patterned tights, and clunky black shoes. The stubble on the shaved part of their head was black; the rest of their hair fell in long, glistening blond waves fastened with a rainbow pin. Both of their dark black eyebrows were threaded with rows of rings. They could have been one of her students. Beth felt a pang so strong it made her wince. Would she see any of her students again? Anyone she loved? Just what was Bene going to do with her?

"We're looking for Bene," Eve said.

The clerk glanced at Regan, then paused with wide eyes. "Oh my goddess! I loved you on Ellen today! Are you seriously going to come out as pan? Please tell me that is not a celebrity stunt to get attention."

"It's not a stunt," Beth said, hoping she was not lying. Regan wouldn't do that.

"Well, if you *are* pan, then we could really use a spokesperson," the clerk lectured, leading Beth and Eve to the back of the tiny shop. "People would pay attention to *your* face, honey! What we do *not* need," they went on, "is another tourist in the queer world, trying to make us a trendy fashion instead of an actual and legitimate way of being."

"I know." Beth winced under a fresh stab of guilt. She *was* a tourist. She was parading around in someone else's skin. A beautiful, internationally famous, universally worshipped skin, with all its genes and its chemical memories and its embedded desires, and she meant to slip out of it as soon as she possibly could.

The clerk opened a narrow door with a sign that said "Loading Dock, Employees Only" and yelled into it. "Bene!"

Eve led the way down a steep, dark, narrow flight of stairs. Beth clung to the railing, her feet not exactly steady. At the bottom, another bright blue door opened into a tiny room filled from floor to ceiling with artifacts, bottles, candles, and tidily labeled packages. Against one wall stood an altar piled with more candles, skulls, painted pictures, and small figures made of cloth and straw. A pungent odor pierced the air, making Beth's stomach heave.

The figure standing in the middle of the room bowed. "*Bonswa,* and welcome to the peristyle." He was a slight man, smaller even than Regan, with gleaming brown skin, enormous eyes, and a crown of cinnamon braids tied back with a scarf. He wore a Bob Marley T-shirt and a pair of flip flops.

Bene straightened and looked into Beth's eyes. "*Bondye,*" he whispered. "It worked."

Beth reached out to cling to a nearby shelf as her knees sagged with relief. He knew. Somehow, just like the Voudou priest and priestess had, he knew she'd been switched.

"It worked too well." Her voice sounded distant, drifting from far away. "I need to turn it back, please." Could he do it here—utter a simple spell, and put Regan Forrester back in her own body?

What on earth would Eve think?

"What worked?" Eve asked suspiciously.

"It was a—" Bene started, but Beth cut him off. "Nothing."

Bene plucked a lit joint from the altar and drew on it. "Kevin was here earlier," he said. "He told me he was getting some things for you."

Fear crawled down Beth's spine like a slimy millipede. "Kevin and I aren't together anymore," she said. "So whatever he was procuring was for himself."

Bene mouthed his joint, watching Beth with wide, considering eyes. "I can't believe it worked. You tried so many times—" He shook his head. "What is it like?"

"It's freaking me out," Beth said. "And also, I don't think it's going to last much longer on its own. She kept telling me it would wear off, but . . ." She glanced at Eve.

Eve moved closer. "What's going to wear off?"

Bene took a puff, holding Beth's eyes. "Eve, *ti chouchou*, could you take your beautiful self upstairs and ask Gladys for a pen? I need one."

Eve wavered. "Regan wants to know why you call yourself Bene."

"Because I call only the spirits that serve the good." Bene blew a perfectly formed ring of smoke into the air before Beth's face. "Understand?"

Beth nodded, her throat closing. Bene glanced at Eve and tilted his head toward the stairs.

"*Pa gen pwoblem*," he said softly in Creole.

Eve huffed and stomped up the stairs. As soon as

the door closed, Bene moved to a rack of neatly labeled containers. "She has to agree to it for the transfer to succeed," he said.

"She will. She does," Beth lied. Bene looked at her a long moment, as if reading her mind. Beth gestured to Regan's willowy, perfect body. "Seriously. Who wouldn't want all this?"

"I thought she'd want back. Once she saw the other side." Chuckling to himself, Bene moved among the tall shelves stacked with strange items, opening and closing drawers.

Beth nodded. The lump in her throat made it impossible to speak. He seemed to know what he was doing. He could help. In a couple of hours she would be back in her own body, in her life, in her Jacuzzi.

If Regan agreed. She was sure, despite what she'd said in the tattoo parlor, that Regan deep down had to want her life back. She needed Beth to fix this for them both.

"What happens if she changes her mind?"

"Then the tie is broken, and the *ti bon ange* floats free," Bene said. He tapped a few flakes of something dried and curled onto the plate. "And if that happens . . ."

"*Zonbi*," Beth whispered, recalling the warning of the priest and priestess.

Bene's eyes narrowed. "They cannot help you," he said as if he saw the image in her head. "Their oaths forbid it. You will have to come back to me. We will try again."

Beth shivered. If her spirit left Regan Forrester's

body and Regan's spirit didn't come back in, Regan would be a body without a soul.

And what of Beth's body, if Regan didn't release it? Would Beth's unhomed spirit flee to Minnesota and howl around the edges of her life, sobbing to be let in?

Just as Cathy's ghost scratched at the window of her old bedroom in Wuthering Heights at the beginning of the novel, scaring the overnight guest out of his skin.

Or maybe both spirits would fly free, and Beth's body would be left a zombie in her own life. How would she take care of her children, in that case? What would happen to Barony? Would she simply go through the motions of the life she knew, performing its daily functions but empty of soul, joy, and purpose?

Wasn't that what she felt she'd been doing before?

Beth's teeth chattered with a sudden chill. Bene brought his plate to the altar and lit a candle. He sang or chanted something under his breath as he rolled the ingredients he'd gathered into a neat, tight cylinder. Then he pulled a pen out of the back pocket of his jeans, took a tiny slip of paper from a cup, and scribbled some words on it. He handed both scraps of paper to Beth.

"You still have the candle and water?"

"There's a glass of water, yes. I think it's evaporating," Beth said.

"Refill it. Tap water's fine." Bene picked up joint, which smelled like plain, garden variety cannabis.

"Burn the herbs, say the words, burn those, too."

Beth looked at the paper. It was written in Haitian Creole, not her classroom French. "Do I need to know what they mean?"

Bene smiled and exhaled a puff of smoke at her. "No."

Beth tucked the precious items into the pocket of her slacks. "Anything else? An—offering?" She gulped, recalling her online search. "Animal sacrifice?"

Bene rolled his eyes. "An offering of food is acceptable. The *lwa* who comes will need to be fortified for the work."

Beth thought back to her refrigerator and hoped there was still food in it. She hadn't exactly planned meals. "What's in the joint?"

"*Datura stramonium.*" Bene tapped ash onto the small plate on the altar. "Be careful with it."

"What?" Eve barked from the doorway. "Zombi cucumber?" She clattered down the stairs, her heels banging on the thin wood. "Regan, you can't take that. It's poisonous."

Beth's hands trembled as she picked up her purse. "I don't have a choice. Bene, what do I owe you?"

She managed to drag Eve back to the car before she erupted. "Want to tell me what's going on, Regan?" Eve hissed, her face taut with tension as she slammed the car door. In the shadowed darkness, her eyes caught the glow of the streetlights. "Why you're messing with a *bokor*, and he's giving you drugs that can kill you?"

Beth's fingers tingled. All of her nerves tingled, come to think of it. Her thoughts were confused, jumpy. It was like Regan's body was trying to eject Beth from her skin.

Or smother her.

"I made a mistake," Beth whispered. "And I have to fix it. You don't have to have any part of this."

"I'm thinking I'd better be part of this," Eve said sharply. "I don't think you have idea what you're doing. How dangerous it is."

Beth watched Los Angeles flash by the window. There was so much of it that she, Beth Barony, would like to have seen. The Chinese theater and the Walk of Fame, with all its memorable names encased in their stars. Beverly Hills and Rodeo Drive.

She'd like to peek at the stars at the Griffith Observatory and eat funnel cake at Santa Monica Pier. See the things the tourists saw, and then, like the tourists, go back to the familiar life she'd briefly escaped from. How beautiful, how sacred that life seemed to her now.

"Is this Kevin's idea?" Eve demanded, her voice full of wrath.

A cold brush of alarm prickled Beth's neck at the mention of Kevin. Beth laid her aching head against the seat back. "It's my doing. I mean it, Eve. I'm fixing something. I can't back out now."

She didn't have the option of staying in Regan Forrester's beautiful, movie-star body. It was kicking her out.

The hallway outside the apartment was empty of

Kevin's things. Every last bag was gone, the carpet undented, neat as a pin. Beth's prickle of alarm intensified.

"It just occurred to me that Kevin still has a key. To the building, and possibly this apartment."

Eve had her phone out before Beth finished the sentence. "I'll talk to the doorman, see if he was here." She gave Beth that piercing look again. "And then I'm coming back here to check on you."

Beth gave her a wobbly smile. "What about that famous yacht party?"

"Satya will have another one."

"I'll be fine," Beth said. "Really. You should go."

"I'll be right back," Eve said firmly. "Don't do anything until I get here."

The moment Eve left, Beth wanted to summon her back. She didn't want to be alone during this. She didn't know what she was doing. Something could go wrong. And she was horribly afraid she was about to yank Regan Forrester back into the last place on earth she wanted to be.

She wondered how many times Regan had tried the spell. What was she trying to escape? Fame? The constant cameras? Her mom?

Kevin. Another ripple of fear made the hair on the back of Beth's neck stand up. Regan was afraid of Kevin.

But she'd fixed that. Beth had a restraining order. Regan would be safe now. She could come home.

And so could Beth.

The apartment felt haunted and empty. When Beth turned on a lamp, the space seemed to quiver.

She took out the things Bene had given her and left her purse and keys by the door. She wanted everything where Regan could find it when she came back.

The bedroom, too, felt eerie, waiting. Beth was as nervous as the first day of school. She took the glass of water off the dressing table to refill it and then, on second thought, pulled a clean glass out of the cabinet. No need to insult the spirits with used glassware.

There was no food left in the refrigerator, not even leftover pad Thai. Tamara must have been hungry. There was, however, a fresh plastic container of green goo. Beth poured some into a glass and sniffed. It smelled like kale and some other pungent, weedy green that made her stomach churn.

The spirits would be disappointed when she couldn't even offer real, whole foods. But there wasn't time to correct the error. She would just have to hope that whatever *lwa* came to the aid of a Hollywood actress would not be insulted to receive a healthy juiced meal in a glass as an offering.

She lit the candle and then wondered if she should change her clothes. Would Regan want to find her body in a pantsuit? But she couldn't put on a skimpy negligee like what she'd first woken up in. Eve was coming back, and for another thing, what if something did go wrong and people had to be called in? She didn't want to be Marilyn Monroe, discovered in the nude.

Beth put a hand to her throbbing temple. This

had to be Regan in her head, worried about how she looked to everyone. Needing to appear to advantage, even in distress. But no, what was her mother's advice: always wear pretty underwear, in case there's an accident. Maybe her mother learned this lesson from Marilyn Monroe.

Beth's chest hurt as she arranged all the pieces as Bene had instructed. If the spell didn't work and her spirit popped out of Regan's body but not back into her own, where would she go? Would she be reunited with people she'd lost?

Maybe she'd see her mom again. They could travel the world as they'd always said they would, as disembodied spirits. Maybe Grandma could come with. It might be less painful to be cast out of her body, exiled from her world, if her spirit were lying on a beach in French Riviera, skimming the ancient ruins of Egypt, diving the Great Barrier Reef.

Beth swallowed a giddy giggle. She had to pull herself together.

No, she had to get out of here.

She sent a text to Beth Barony's phone. *I'm starting it now.*

No answer.

She pulled out the stool of the dressing table and sat. Bene said Regan needed to be willing. But Beth hadn't been willing, not really. She hadn't asked to be yanked out of her life, and if she had—if the spell had operated on some deep subconscious desire, working on her while Beth was asleep—then it could certainly serve to yank Regan Forrester back into her body. She couldn't honestly wish to give up youth, fame, talent, opportunity, and this sexiest-woman-alive body for Beth Barony's middle-aged, middle class, middle America life.

But Regan had cast all that off in the first place, wanted something else so badly she was willing to dabble with spirits and spells. Maybe Regan really was done with this life. Maybe Beth needed to learn to live in this glamorous skin, make something of the girl's opportunities. Be a good example. Use her gifts—

The pain in her head felt like a chainsaw slicing through her skull. *Out.* She needed out now.

She laid the cell phone on the dressing table, lit the joint Bene had rolled for her, and set it on the small plate to burn. The acrid odor clawed inside her nose, stinging tears from her eyes. It smelled like burning grass and vinegar. She unwrapped the scrap of paper and read the words Bene had written. They rolled off her tongue in a voice not hers, large, deep, full of the weight of centuries.

Suddenly she wasn't alone in the room.

21 • THE SPELL

Burning smoke filled the room, forming columns of swirling air. Beth couldn't see through the tears in her eyes. Her head felt as if it floated free from her body. Her limbs swam through air thick with fumes. Her eyes played tricks on her. It looked as if the room were filled with people, crowds of people, but they seemed so far away, at distances the room could not possibly hold.

The walls had disappeared and she was on an open plain in a large square of trodden grass beneath a huge gnarled tree. Flames from a bonfire leapt into the air, showering sparks and an odor that needled into her brain and skin. Drums beat in her ears, rolling, tidal, a heartbeat pulsing blood through her awakened body. She felt ten feet tall. She felt invincible.

She was curled up on the ground, arms clutched around her belly, writhing in pain. Her innards were bursting open. This was worse than childbirth. She felt split from stem to stern, pulled apart at the roots. Her heart pounded in her chest, her throat clogged, her head rolled in torment.

She saw dancers far away, stomping and singing out the words she had read, shaking their heads and their painted faces, shaking beads and rattles in a rising, deafening cadence. Heat showered through her, bolting up from her core. A body crouched over her, a man with a wide grin on his demon face, his eyes painted red from the firelight.

"Not so sassy now, are ya?" the man sneered.

"Kevin," Beth gasped. "Help me."

"Sure, now you need me." Kevin laughed and the sound split her head apart. "Bitch."

She was curled up on Regan Forrester's plush carpet, in Regan Forrester's apartment, not on some faraway African landscape. The silk of her pantsuit scraped her raw, over-sensitized skin. The light hurt her eyes. The floor rocked. "Kevin—something's happening . . ."

"About time. Did you take it?"

"Take what?" She gasped at the stabbing pain in her head. The drums pounded louder now, the sound of chanting and rattling and stomping feet growing enormous, coming at her from all sides. Kevin didn't seem to notice them. Lights leapt and cavorted on the edge of her vision. She closed her eyes against the burning brightness.

Kevin shook her shoulders. "Did you take it!" he shouted.

"I didn't—take anything—" Oh God, her head was going to fall off. Her chest was splitting open. The smoke filled her nose, her mouth, her lungs. She was choking. His eyes were red and mad, filled with hatred. He held a glass toward her, green, the liquid bubbling and boiling like a cauldron.

Cool. It felt cool against her fevered skin, her lips. "Drink it," he commanded.

She drank. The cool would help the burning in her throat. But the drink tasted like metal, like acid. Like the clouds of killing chemicals farmers sprayed on their fields in the summer to keep away pests.

Her stomach refused to take it in. Beth vomited the liquid, choking, and Kevin slapped her across the face so hard that her neck creaked.

"Bitch!" he screamed. "You have to take it!"

Bands of hot iron clamped her temples, pressing against the throbbing pain. Her heart galloped like a frenzied animal trying to burst out of her chest. Gasping, on her hands and knees, Beth crawled away from him. The other figures would give her protection.

She saw a woman walking toward her, tall as the sun, her skin gleaming like burnished mahogany, her eyes glowing embers. Feathers, beads, and shiny metals winked and waved in her long braids, coiling around her like serpents as she walked.

She wore a tight wrap dress with strings of beads and gems hanging from her wrists, neck, and waist. Bracelets of gold coiled up her forearms and calves, and her feet were bare. Her body was strong and pulsing with life, lit with a terrifying radiance. She looked down at Beth with a face curious and impassive, the goddess regarding mortals from on high.

"Erzulie." Somehow Beth knew her name. It came to her out of the fog of her mind, the clamor of the drums and the dancing. One of the most powerful of the *lwa*, the protector of women and children.

"I answer," the goddess said, her voice like a waterfall in full spate.

"Get out of here!" Kevin swore. His voice sounded amplified, like many voices speaking at once. "I'm the one who will command her!"

"You will not!" the goddess roared. "What you do is forbidden."

At least, that's what Beth thought she said. She floated half out of her body—Regan's body. She saw a woman crouched on the floor like a wounded animal, swaying back and forth. But she could also see around her, for leagues, crowds of spirits with decorated faces and glowing eyes, pressing close and curious.

Erzulie raised a hand in a sweeping gesture and the demon man with the red eyes fell back, howling. He gathered himself like an animal ready to spring, and she made the gesture again, more forceful this time. The demon stumbled backwards through the doorway and somehow Beth knew he was gone. Perhaps the spirits had carried him away.

The goddess-woman stepped closer, and Beth cowered. She didn't want to be possessed by a spirit, any spirit. There wasn't enough space inside; her skin was too tight, squeezing her out, and yet she clung blindly to the human form, afraid of being cast into nothingness.

"I'm . . . poisoned," Beth gasped, still on her hands and knees. "Really—bad trip."

"I told you so." The goddess had Eve's voice, Eve's eyes. "What do I do?"

"Sherice. Nurse. Call Sherice."

Beth sucked in air, but the room was filled with burning smoke. It was everywhere. It smelled sweet now, like a cool breeze in summer. Her heart clenched and gulped.

The goddess held a small purple rectangle—cell phone. Regan's.

Beth stabbed a number into it and gathered every last scrap of sense.

"Sherice!" she cried when her friend answered. "Sher. Need you."

"Who is this?"

"Beth." No, strange voice. Sherice wouldn't recognize her. "Friend of—Beth. Beth—" Her throat closed as her tongue choked her. Her head was drifting away.

Erzulie-Eve tapped the speaker button and spoke calmly. "Hi, Sherice? You're a nurse? I need your help. I'm here with a friend, I think she was poisoned or had a drug overdose, and I don't know what to do."

"What did she take?" Sherice's voice sharpened into professional mode. Faced with a crisis, she would solve the main problem first. Beth wheezed and leaned toward the voice, toward safety. "Do you see any bottles, any needles, anything in a bag, or a—"

"*Datura*," Erzulie-Eve said. "We call it zombi cucumber. I think you call it jimsonweed here."

"Oh, holy mother." Sherice's voice rose. "That's a nightshade, extremely toxic. Did she eat it or smoke it?"

"Just breathed the smoke, I think." The goddess figure looked urgently at Beth. "Regan—did he make you drink?"

"Spit—out," Beth managed. She narrowed her eyes against the light.

Erzulie-Eve glowed with supernatural bright-ness. Behind her, closer than the rest of the pressing crowds, Beth saw two tall, powerful figures emerging from pillars of smoke. The woman wore a long robe and a headwrap and a thick collar of brilliant beads. The man was older, silver-haired, also in a long robe. Both held up their arms, chanting in a low hum, while a circle of figures around them danced and swayed.

The light burned so brightly. Beth whimpered. How did the priest and priestess from the temple get here? Did they guess what she was about and come to stop her from meddling with unnatural forces, to protect the balance between the earthly and spirit world as they were sworn to do?

Sherice would save her. Her friend's voice was so confident, so dear. Beth curled around the phone, letting the nonsense words flow through her head.

"The actives in that will be atropine and scopolamine," Sherice rapped out. "They're anti-cholinergics. It's possible the effects will wear off in a few hours, but we can't be sure. When you call the first responders, tell them she'll need intravenous physostigmine." She repeated the word slowly. "They may know how to administer it."

Erzulie-Eve nodded along to all of this, as if locking it in her mind. Beth rolled onto her back, feeling flames crawl over her. She was rising out of her skin.

"Going—through the looking—glass now," she breathed. She watched the two forms of the *hougan* and *manbo*, rippling, ethereal, awe-inspiring. Their chant lifted her, held her, as if guiding her. As if they had come to help. Behind them stood ranks of shimmering forms, spirits, ancestors. Come to welcome her into their world.

"This is a California number," Sherice said suddenly. "How do you know Beth?"

Beth blinked against the blazing light. Her heart leapt and spun. She knew why this wasn't working. She flopped onto her belly, struggling to her hands and knees.

"Joanie," she gasped. "Sher—call Joan—go to house. Beth's house. Back porch—Jacuzzi—wine."

She whimpered as her head split open. She felt a warm, steady hand on her forehead.

"Stay with me," Eve whispered. "You're going to be okay."

Beth peered at her, narrowing her eyes against the light. The tidal wave poured through her opening head, while her heart spilled out of her chest.

"Tell everyone—love them," Beth panted. "Have to—go."

Eve muttered something in Creole. It sounded like a blessing. Beth saw the rising pocket of dark and rolled herself into it.

22 • THE CONSEQUENCES

Much, much later, Beth rolled herself out of the pocket, climbing toward a pinprick of light.

With every step her light, airy body grew heavier. Her limbs felt weighted, her body sheathed and thick. But her skin did not feel on fire. Her head did not pound with the rhythm of drums. Her hands were stuck under something, pressed down on a fabric surface, but she could wiggle her toes.

She moved her mouth in a smile and felt her lips crack. "Not dead."

"She's awake." A male voice, hoarse, deep. It came from beside her. A pressure on her hand. The scent of Irish Spring, clean and delicious. Timothy was here, at her bedside. She lay in a bed. She heard beeping.

"Have a body," Beth said gratefully, wiggling her toes again. She squeezed the hands that held hers.

"Girl, you are so lucky," said a woman's voice. "You gave us the scare of our days."

A voice like velvet, luscious as a popsicle. Must be Eve holding her other hand. Beth thought about opening her eyes. She listened for a moment to her steady heartbeat, the blood rushing through soft tissues, through muscle and tendon and skin, from lungs to heart to everywhere between.

What a brilliant, delicate machine, the human body. How glad she was to be in it. "Not a zombie," she said gratefully. She was so happy to be in a body—any body—she might cry. She wasn't dead or lost, a keening spirit. She had friends at her bedside. That meant a great deal.

"You would be a zombie if I'd been any later," a third voice snapped. "You're lucky you didn't slide under the water!"

That didn't sound like Tamara. "Water? Where was there—?" Beth opened her eyes.

Her heart stopped beating.

She was in a hospital bed, in a hospital room. A blue curtain cut the room in half. She lay under a blanket but could see the bumps of her feet. Could hear the machine beeping at her ear.

Joan held her hand, a worn, worried look on her face. Her lipstick was smudged and one half of her shirt collar poked up into her hair. The inside of her wrist was flaming red around a brand new tattoo.

"You know hydrocodone knocks you out," Joan barked. "And then to wash it down with wine? You could have killed yourself, Beth!"

"We'll know when the blood test comes back if there was anything else."

Sherice stood beside her, hanging a new IV bag on the tree. Her braids were wrapped into a tight bun and she wore her scrubs with the green dinosaurs romping across a blue background. Her name badge and a stethoscope dangled around her neck.

She leaned over and peered into Beth's eyes. "No mydriasis. That's the freaky big pupil thing. Common side effect of psychotropics."

"Sherice." Beth's voice scratched her throat. "Joan. God, am I glad to see you."

Their eyes slid to Beth's other side. She looked up from the needle taped to her arm and followed their gaze. Barony, his face shadowed with stubble, his eyes irritated and red, clenched his fist around her hand and held it up to his mouth.

"Hi, honey," Beth said. Tears slid from her eyes. "I was so worried I would never see you again."

His shoulders slumped. "I knew we should have tossed that bottle out. After what happened the last time you took one for a migraine—"

"Forgot," she whispered, her voice scratching in her throat. "Stupid. I wasn't thinking."

A laugh scraped out, but it sounded mangled. Had Regan been trying to knock herself out or trying to kill her? All to make sure Beth couldn't yank her back to her real life?

Her gaze roamed over all three beloved faces. She gripped the hands holding hers as hard as she could. "Hated—being away from you," she rasped. "Accident. Honest."

She hoped so. Her head felt heavy, and she let it rest on the pillow. There was something terribly urgent that she needed to do, and she couldn't recall what it was. "Haven't—been myself the last couple of days," she said feebly.

To say the least. She wanted so badly to explain what had happened to her, but saying it here, now, in a hospital bed—she'd find herself on suicide watch, or worse.

Danger. The warnings swirled to her consciousness. What was it she needed to do?

Warn—warn who? About what?

"I'm supposed to be the reckless one." Joan poked her in the arm. "You have a husband and kids to think about."

"Midlife crisis," Sherice said. "Or perimenopause."

"No!" Beth yelped. She looked at her husband. "Barony, I—if I've . . . seemed different . . . " She had no idea what to say.

The tips of his ears turned pink. "You certainly made the most of this birthday." His hand tightened around hers. "But no more drinking in the hot tub, okay? New house rule."

"One glass, max," Beth promised. She let out her breath in a long exhale. Her body felt battered, as if she'd been through a storm. Her leg muscles felt sore and if she lay too long like this, her back would get stiff. Her hair was probably a mess and she certainly was not wearing makeup. She wasn't wearing anything, in fact, but a thin hospital gown. She shifted against the sheets. No underwear.

That made the tips of her ears heat as well. The one time her mother's advice would have come in useful, and Regan didn't know to heed it.

Regan. Where was she? Beth sat bolt upright with a gasp. Joan and Barony gripped her hands.

"I—uh, have to go to the bathroom," Beth flailed.

Joan shot a glare at Sherice. "Can't you give her a bedpan?"

"Uh-uh, it'll be good for her to get up and move around. Want me to bring your IV, hon?"

"Where's my phone?" Beth asked, looking around desperately.

"You need your phone to go the bathroom?" Joan accused her.

"Um—I want to make sure the kids didn't text." She was wasting time. Where was Regan?

In California, where Beth had summoned her back to the apartment where her boyfriend was trying to kill her.

"I didn't call the kids." Barony looked guilty. "I didn't want them to worry."

"Just a quick check-in." Beth struggled to lift her legs over the bed, with Sherice's help. She no longer had Regan Forrester's lithe, strong body. She had forty-two-year-old bones again, stretchy skin, muscles that weren't as limber as they were twenty years ago. God, she loved every inch of this creaky old mess.

Had she been so desperate to get back to Beth's life that she put Regan's life in jeopardy?

Joan found her phone, and Sherice wheeled the IV tree into the bathroom with her. Beth watched them through a crack in the door while she dialed and waited.

Barony sat back in his chair, rubbing a hand over his stubbled face. She'd interrupted his meeting. She'd called Joan away from whatever she was doing. Sherice was likely on loan from the pediatric floor and would have to head back up there soon. Beth would have to teach tomorrow hung over from whatever Regan had done to her, and she had nothing for a lesson plan. She'd have to follow whatever stellar fun Regan Forrester had delivered for her class earlier that day.

She hadn't been able to beat Regan Forrester at the girl's own life, and she wouldn't be able to live up to Regan Forrester's masquerade as Beth Barony. It was back to the same old Beth again, same habits, same ingrained responses, same defeats, same dreams.

But they all felt entirely fresh to her, like a newly discovered paradise. A precious history she hadn't known how to truly appreciate until she very nearly lost it for good. She wanted to explain all this to her friends, to Barony, try to make them understand how glorious and beautiful everything seemed, how dizzyingly grateful she was to have all this.

Regan deserved that, too. The phone rang and rang as Beth clutched the instrument and prayed to every deity she knew, the ones from her childhood and the ones she had just met, that Regan Forrester was safe.

* * *

"If you're calling for Regan, this is a bad time." Eve sounded irritated, her voice distracted and strained.

Beth swallowed hard. "I really need to talk with her. It's important."

A long pause, then Eve's voice again, distant. "A Minnesota number—I don't know who. You want to take it?"

Tamara murmured something, probably offering to take charge and sort everything out. Beth heaved a sigh of relief. Regan wasn't alone.

For a moment she couldn't place the next voice; it sounded different from outside her head. "I'll take it. Give me a minute." Another pause. "I'm going to the bathroom."

Beth slumped onto the stool in the shower. Regan was alive. Regan was back in her body. She sounded as wrecked as Beth felt.

"Are you okay?" Beth whispered when she heard the door close on Regan's end. She hoped her friends weren't listening at the door of her bathroom. Sherice wouldn't, Barony wouldn't, but Joan would.

"No. No, I am not okay." Regan's voice rose. "How are *you*?"

"In the hospital, actually. Turns out my body reacts badly to hydrocodone. Please tell me, Regan, that you weren't trying—you didn't mean to—"

"Oh, my God. No. It was just my head hurt so much. And there was an old prescription in your medicine cabinet."

"From when Drew had his wisdom teeth out a year or two ago," Beth said. Regan didn't need an explanation, but Beth felt like she had to keep her on the phone. She had to make this okay.

"I swear I wasn't trying to kill you." Regan sounded defeated, her voice hoarse and raspy.

"I wasn't trying to kill you, either."

Beth felt like crying. She was alive. They were both alive, back in their proper bodies, the good little angel zipped up back inside the big good angel to which it belonged. The balance was restored. Beth had the feeling there had been some powerful forces helping them transition.

Beth pulled her fingers through her hair. It was a

tangled mess. Regan did not sound like she was bursting with joy to be back in her life.

Because she knew, or at least suspected, that Kevin had been trying to kill her, and she'd been trying to avoid that by any means possible.

"Where is he?" she croaked.

"Kevin? He ran. Eve told them he attacked you when she called 911."

"I'm so, so sorry, Regan," Beth said. "I forgot he'd have a key."

She didn't know what else to say. She wanted them both to be where they belonged, but she wanted them both to be safe.

"Why is Timothy Kay in my hospital room?" Regan whispered. "Is he here about my contract?"

"No." Beth swallowed a laugh. "I think he cares about you. You're in the hospital, too?"

"Yeah, Eve brought me. She told the responders Kevin poisoned me."

"He broke the emergency protective order," Beth said. "I can't believe it. Regan—you can't go back there until he's caught."

"Of course I can't go back there!" Regan yelled. "I tried telling you that! I was out of there, I was away from him, and then you had to—" The hoarse bellow dissolved into sobs.

Beth curled a hand into the thin fabric of her hospital gown. "Come to Eden Prairie," she blurted. "Come stay with me."

She would have smacked herself in the forehead if her head didn't still feel so heavy and strange. What was she thinking? She hadn't been able to fix

Regan's life for her while she was in it. In fact, she'd made a spectacular mess, and then yanked Regan right back into the center of it. *Sure, Beth. She's going to come to Eden Prairie and let you make things all better. Because you did such a fantastic job while you were on site.*

"I know it sounds weird," Beth babbled. "But Tamara's kids are sick, so you can't stay there. It's a lot to ask of Eve or Timothy, and if you stayed with your mom you'd just be taking care of her. But no one would look for you here. You've seen the guest room, and Barony—"

Barony would think she had gone absolutely off the rails. And Joan and Sherice already had her on a suicide watch. She could sense the looks they were exchanging, the furtive whispers behind the closed door.

Beth swallowed a sob. She wanted so badly for Regan to forgive her. "You could come sit in on my class. And we can soak in the Jacuzzi every night."

A long, long silence followed, filled with some rustling, the small quiet blip of a machine. *Idiot!* Beth scolded herself. Regan was done with her. She'd caused the girl nothing but trouble. Yet Beth had the nagging feeling that something between them wasn't finished.

"And Kevin couldn't find you here," she added lamely. "You'd be safe for a while, at least."

Regan let out a long sigh. "How soon can that guest room be ready?"

23 • THE GUEST

Sherice stretched out her hand and admired the silver decals on the fuchsia background of her nails. "I made a good choice."

Joan leaned back in the massage chair, swirling her feet through the pool of warm water. "You're the only one of us who could pull it off." Her gaze slid guiltily to the fourth woman with them. "Though I guess *she* could."

"I like this," Beth said. She held her arms out while on each side of her chair a stylist painted henna tattoos on her palms. "I could get these all over my body."

"Only because there are no needles." Regan Forrester laughed. "Honestly, Beth. You'll never be able to get fillers. Or Botox."

"Fortunately, in my line of work, I don't need fillers or Botox," Beth replied. "The more ancient I appear, the more my students will respect me. Studies show."

"Does it hurt?" Joan asked. "Botox?"

"Joan!" Regan exclaimed. "I do not have Botox on my face! I'm only twenty-four!"

"Of course you don't," Joan said. "Sorry. When you're our age, though . . ."

"I'll save it for twenty-six," Regan said candidly. The nail technician tapped her knee and she lifted one perfectly shaped foot out of the water. "Want to know what does hurt? Breast implants."

All three of them looked at Regan's chest. She

wore a tight T-shirt that outlined her absolutely perfect breasts. She threw her shoulders back, giving them a better view.

"I totally thought they were real," Beth marveled.

"My mom chose the best surgeon. They were my sixteenth birthday present."

"I'm thinking of some," Joan mused. "For my fiftieth."

Sherice jiggled her bosom. "Want some of my girls? Be nice not to have a backache all the time."

All four women laughed, until another young woman approached them. She'd been getting a pedicure with her mom, nose in her phone the entire time, but now she crept across the salon to the chairs where they sat while her mom paid and chatted with the cashier in Korean. The girl could be one of Beth's students, young, self-conscious, just learning how brutally the world could judge her. Beth smiled in welcome, but the girl only had eyes for their guest.

"Excuse me? I'm so sorry, but are you Regan Forrester?"

Regan turned and smiled easily at her. "You guessed. I was sure no one would recognize me in Minnesota." She gave her breathy, movie-star laugh.

"Oh my gosh, that's just—could I—would you mind—could I take a picture with you?" the girl gushed.

"I'll do it." Joan held out her hand.

"Thanks, but I know my good side," Regan said.

She took the girl's phone and leaned in for a selfie. Her hair was pulled back in a ponytail, she wore minimal makeup, and she was dressed in a pair of ripped jeans and a faded shirt. But Beth had seen her get ready that morning and knew even the casual look was carefully curated to look easy, natural, tossed together. Regan Forrester had to be ready at all times for display, even when she was out getting her nails done with the girls.

Regan put her head next to the other girl's, face tilted just right, and they both did a duckface, pursing their lips, sucking in their cheeks. Then Regan paused.

"Why are we making that goofy face? Let's just give our biggest smiles. Wow, look at your smile! You're gorgeous. Such beautiful skin."

Both of them made big, mugging grins at the phone screen, and Regan snapped the picture. The girl made some grateful noises and clutched her phone. "If you do a filter, I want panda ears," Regan called as the girl scurried away.

Beth looked down at her emerging tattoos. Regan's gesture surprised her, but in a good way. In a way that made tears rise to her eyes.

Sherice chuckled. "I suppose you get that all the time."

Regan shrugged and leaned back while the technician worked on her foot. "I'll never get used to all the attention. There's always that feeling of who, me?"

Joan held out a foot for a technician to scrub. "I can't figure out how you got to know Beth. And how on earth she got you to come out here for a visit."

Regan glanced at Beth and they both grinned.

"Um..." Regan started.

"I emailed her," Beth said. "The night of my birthday, after we saw her movie, and you told us, Joanie, about that interview in *People*. I felt sad that she didn't have many female friends. I had too much wine, and I emailed her and told her she should come to Minnesota because I have the best girlfriends in the entire world. And here she is."

Regan laughed. "Yeah, something like that," she said. "Plus, I was going through a rough patch, and I needed to get away." She sighed with pleasure as the technician scrubbed her foot. "It feels good to be around people I don't have to pay to be nice to me."

"You have people like that in your life," Beth said. "A couple, at least."

Regan held her eyes. It was good to look at the girl's famous face, her classic features and sparkling green eyes, and know her spirit was in residence. Instead of looking in the mirror seeing Beth Barony trying to get out.

"I realize that," Regan said softly.

"But not Kevin McDonald." Joan winced as the technician worked off a callus. "What *happened* to him? We all had such a crush on him in *Waiting for Dell*."

"Not me," Beth said immediately. "I had a crush on the chess nerd."

"And I had a thing for the funny Black friend who had no idea how to relate to women," Sherice said. "Which explains *my* romantic history."

They laughed, but Regan made a face.

"Well, I had a crush on Kevin, too, and I think

that's why I kept giving him another chance." She sighed. "Except now he broke my emergency protective order, and my mom wants to charge him with attempted murder after it turns out he was poisoning me through this diet he made me try."

"What in the ever-loving world," Joan exclaimed.

"I know." Regan's laugh sounded forced. "He knew I wanted to leave him, so he was trying some kind of mind control experiment. He got it from this story in Haitian folklore about this guy who could make zombies. You know my dad's Haitian," Regan said proudly.

"Wait, I read about this in my pharmacology class," Sherice said. "There was this doctor who claimed he could control peoples' minds, turn them into zombies using tetrodotoxin. It's the neurotoxin produced by the pufferfish. And some other drug was involved—Datura, I think." She turned a quizzical gaze on Beth.

Beth rushed in before Sherice could start piecing things together. "How is your mom?" she asked Regan.

"She finally decided to start a twelve-step program," Regan said. "She said after the last time we fought, she thought I'd never talk to her again, but when I called her out of the blue and invited her to do something with me—well, she said she'd missed me so much, and she owed it to me to get help."

Beth concentrated on the designs emerging on her hands. So she'd done one good thing for Regan, at least.

"I hope they put Kevin McDonald in jail for a century," Beth said. "Doesn't your director have a big crush on you? Timothy Kay?"

"I do like older men," Regan said with a smile. "But Timothy Kay? I'm not sure. I might want a little time to myself for now."

Joan broke the moment by laughing. "Regan Forrester, in our town," she exclaimed. "Beth, what did Barony say when you told him *People's* most beautiful woman was coming to visit?"

"He was embarrassed," Beth said. "And the next day he spent an hour at the gym. And then he was worried that we didn't have nice enough sheets in the spare bedroom and made me go out and buy a new set. I told him he's not allowed to fall in love with her."

Beth glanced at Regan. The situation with Barony was something she still hadn't thought through when she was picking Regan Forrester up from the Minneapolis airport and bringing her to school, like a very memorable show and tell.

It certainly transformed her class, having Regan Forrester among them. Over the course of a week, she'd done with Dicken's *Tale of Two Cities* and Virginia Woolf's *Orlando* the same thing she'd done with *Wuthering Heights,* having the students act out scenes and inhabit characters. Beth's class evals for this summer were going to be the best ever.

But she felt like Regan had transformed, too. She didn't seem sad, or anxious, or frightened, or stressed. She'd settled very easily into Beth's quiet life—no surprise—but with the added benefit of having her own movie-star-perfect body and gorgeously memorable face this time.

Of course, she could be hiding everything. She *was* an actor.

"Barony's really sweet. He would never cheat on you." Regan watched the technician sweep pale color over her toenails. "You're really lucky, Beth, to have a guy that devoted. He would do anything for you."

"He is sweet," Beth said. A pang of guilt stabbed her. She had the best guy in the world, and she'd been taking him for granted for at least ten years. She'd allowed them both to fall into a rut. It had taken Regan Forrester to shake them out of it.

The night she came home from the hospital, Barony watched her walk through the house, touching everything as if she'd forgotten what it looked like. She smiled at their wedding pictures, the walls of photographs showing the kids growing up, the frames of them together, laughing. After she walked onto the back porch to look at the summer flowers, smell the clean air, and look at the beautiful spangle of stars in their bed of black velvet, she'd turned to find Barony standing at the sliding door, nearly in tears.

"I swear I was not trying to kill myself," Beth promised him, stepping into his arms.

"Then what *were* you doing?" He held her stiffly, as if afraid she might break, but turned his face into her hair.

"Getting a wake-up call," Beth had said.

"I suppose Drew's already in love with you," Joan

said to Regan, propping her painted toenails on the footrest to dry.

Regan smiled. "He's really sweet, too."

"He took first place in both his events at the final meet," Beth reported, "because he knew Regan was in the audience. And his picture with her will be in a national magazine, so you can imagine how proud he is."

She was still impressed with how friendly Regan was with Beth's friends and family, how natural and at ease she'd been in all the crowds. In Hollywood, her part as Regan Forrester, rising actress, was a 24/7 reality show. But Beth had the feeling that the real Regan Forrester—the girl she'd gotten to know on the phone, the young woman she'd come to know from the inside out—was the person with them now.

Beth liked her a lot better this way.

"I hope you know we won't hold you to the promise of going to prom if Drew can't find a date," she said.

Regan smiled. "He'll find a date. You have good kids, Beth. I'm looking forward to picking Abby up from her camp this weekend."

"She said the dance was a lot of fun," Beth responded. "Thanks to some good advice I gave her."

"Maybe you can talk to my daughter, too," Sherice suggested. "She's—um—"

"Not confused," Joan said sternly.

"No, just not straight," Sherice said. "But I think she's worried that I'll be anxious for her. And you—

well, not to put you on the spot ..."

"No, that's fine. I'm a big question mark myself," Regan said. "I'm going to tell her, though, that I hate labels. I don't think you have to define your gender or sexuality. And you don't have to be defined by it, either. You should just be who you are and not apologize to anyone for it."

Beth blinked as those words dove through her, smarting like a slap to the face.

"Just be who you are," she managed to say.

It was one of those catchphrases she heard tossed around so often that she'd forgotten what it really meant. Funny how she'd needed Regan Forrester to come into her life and show her that being Beth Barony—no frills, no superpowers, no special deal Beth Barony—was actually the only thing she ever needed to be.

Regan met her eyes as if there was no one else in the room. "I'm glad I can finally say that," she answered. "I have spent so, so much time worrying whether other people like me. It got so bad that I couldn't even stand to be in my own body."

"What happened?" Sherice asked curiously.

Regan looked at her freshly manicured nails. "I tried being someone else for a while. Someone who actually felt secure in her own skin. Who was accepted and admired and loved for exactly who she is."

The smile only stretched one side of her mouth. "It felt really good." She paused, then took a deep breath, lifting her eyes to meet Beth's.

"And I decided I wanted that for myself. To learn

how to feel comfortable in my skin. As me."

Beth's eyes misted with tears, and she blinked them away.

"Regan was my birthday wish," she realized suddenly.

Joan laughed. "What?"

"Remember? Sherice told me I needed more excitement in my life." Beth's grin stretched from ear to ear as she looked at her friends. "Well, Regan made that happen. In ways you really would not believe."

Regan joined in their laughter, her smile full of mesmerizing beauty. "You're welcome," she said, "but, oh Beth, just you wait. I'm not finished with you yet."

24 · FINALE

Beth stood once more in Regan Forrester's bedroom, wearing a designer gown. She twirled before the full-length mirror, laughing at herself. "I cannot believe how amazing I look."

"I know! I am *so* good at this." Regan, on her hands and knees, crept around the floor-length hemline, steaming out one last stubborn crease. "Whenever I give up acting, I'm going to become a personal stylist. I did great with your wardrobe, right?"

"Really great," Beth confirmed. "Even my students were impressed."

Eve, pinning up her hair at the dressing table, turned to glance at Regan. "You're giving up acting?"

"Not anytime soon. I have two more *Visitors* films on my contract, and I like the scripts we're being offered. I'm not typecast as the beautiful dummy anymore."

Beth sensed an undercurrent in their look, which lasted a beat too long. There was something yet unresolved between these two.

"You were never the beautiful dummy," Beth said loyally, even though that's exactly what she had thought of Regan Forrester before she knew her. Before she saw the world through her eyes.

"I was." Regan sat back on her heels, sending Beth a look full of meaning. "But I gave a couple of great interviews where everyone said I was so articulate and intelligent, and Ellen told everyone I was really smart, so now..." She shrugged. "I don't have to be the dummy anymore."

Beth held still as Regan turned her this way and that, arranging the fall of her skirt. "How's Mom doing in rehab?" she asked.

"Great, actually! She says it's going to stick this time. She really came through for me after the whole Kevin thing." Regan's green eyes glowed with mischief as she glanced up at Beth. "How's co-teaching the drama class?"

Beth laughed. "Great, thanks to your advice. Keep it coming."

It was still surreal to her that she and Regan had remained friends after their wild experience. Regan Forrester, hot young Hollywood A-lister, and Beth Barony, middle-aged Midwestern schoolteacher mom. She knew it looked absurd to anyone outside. But after what they'd gone through in each other's lives, there was nothing they couldn't talk about. It was strangely liberating.

Beth submitted to more rearranging, then had to ask. "And how's Timothy?"

Regan's reddened lips twitched. "He's nice," she allowed. "But I don't think he's really interested. Besides, I'm not locking myself down yet. I have to make mortgage payments now, and I like playing house by myself. I feel like I need to get to know me better before I invite anyone else in."

She grinned suddenly, pushing back a coil of sleek black hair that had fallen from its pins. "Did I tell you? I'm learning to cook. I met a private chef."

"Regan, *ti chouchou*, you look absolutely smashing." Eve rose from the dressing table. "And I also think Beth looks great. So maybe you can stop crushing your dress and let Tamara finish your makeup."

"Timothy and Barony have their tuxes and are downstairs with the limo," Tamara reported, coming into the bedroom. "Beth, here are your shoes. Wow, you look terrific! Regan is so good at this. Regan, sweetie, your speech is in your bag." She held up the printed slip of paper. "Don't forget it! You worked so hard."

"Of course I won't forget it! My first big award." Regan came to the dressing table and let Eve fret over her hair while Tamara put the last touches on her makeup. "Are you sure it's for real?"

"It is real," Eve confirmed. "Best short film with a public service message. You're going to get nominated for more awards, now. But tonight you'll have to share the podium with Timothy for the acceptance speech, so don't let him go on too long."

Eve glanced at Beth. "You're the one Regan says should get the credit for this. It's nice that you and your husband could come all the way from Minnesota."

"It's all Regan," Beth said. "But we were delighted to make the trip. I wanted to see more of LA. Today we saw the Walk of Fame *and* the Hollywood sign."

"Beth was my inspiration," Regan said, closing her eyes while Tamara dusted powder over her face. "She's a teacher, you know. In a way I feel like she's the one who made this film." When she opened her eyes, they shone with excitement and joy.

"But I'm still taking the award."

Barony and Timothy Kay stood on the sidewalk in front of Regan's apartment, leaning against the limo and having an animated conversation about the architectural value of the building. Both men fell silent as the women approached. Barony gaped at Regan, gowned in a dazzling sapphire ballgown that brought out her eyes and showed every outline of her figure. Timothy Kay, oddly, stared at Beth.

"You look—wow," Barony said, remembering to compliment his wife.

"Thanks, honey. You too." Beth slid into the seat beside him and tried to make casual conversation with Timothy Kay as they rode to the hotel where the awards ceremony would be held.

Beth found it delightful to walk the red carpet when nobody cared who you were—just another pair in their fancy gown and tux, filling in the crowd scene while the cameras focused on the beautiful people. It was exciting to be part of the glamor and a relief not to be the center of attention.

She grinned when two young women stopped her and asked to photograph the woman who had inspired Regan's short film. She recognized the reporters, Larissa and Koko, both of whom had questioned her as Regan Forrester. They were clearly a couple, and Beth laughed to herself as she stood exactly as they instructed so they could catch her good side.

Regan grabbed Barony's arm to walk the carpet and snuggled into him as the cameras devoured her. She struck one of her sultry starlet poses, backside to the camera, throwing an over-the-shoulder pout, her hand on Barony's chest. The tops of his ears turned red, but his arm crept around her tiny waist.

Beth, walking behind them on Timothy's arm, pasted a smile to her face. What if Barony fell under Regan's spell again? He'd been perfectly well behaved and sensible the two weeks Regan stayed with them, but he also refused to talk about the days of her "mid-life crisis," as he called it. She'd been so grateful that the little 'crisis' hadn't resulted in an unplanned pregnancy that she didn't push him to share details.

What if Barony decided he wanted to be free of his boring wife and kids, his demanding job as junior partner? What if he wanted something more and wasn't telling her, just when Beth had realized that their life was everything she wanted?

"Regan says you're responsible for this."

The deep voice at her ear sent a shiver of delight down Beth's back. She'd tried to limit her time with Timothy, keeping conversation light and informal for precisely this reason.

Her reaction to him wasn't something Regan Forrester felt; it was all Beth.

"I'm a teacher," Beth said, glancing up into his lean, stubbled face. "Keeping kids in school is important to me." At least she hoped he was talking about the film.

They both watched the cameras adore Regan, and Beth's stomach twisted as the actress planted a chaste kiss on Barony's cheek. He looked embarrassed and proud.

"She's such an amazing person," Beth said softly. "You two seem to be on good terms?"

Timothy's eyes were remote, shadowed. Beth smelled Irish Spring. She forced herself not to lean closer.

"Friendly terms. She's a little young," Timothy said in a low voice. "For a while, she was acting like—well, someone more mature."

His eyes turned to Beth. "She knew all the classic Golden Era films. She cooked me food. She even helped at a soup kitchen. Now she seems—well, not quite the person she was when we were filming *The Visitors*. There's more depth to her than I thought, but still . . . young."

His voice deepened as he looked carefully at Beth, his gaze sweeping her elaborately styled hair, the elegant gown, the makeup that Tamara had professionally applied. "I hope you'll forgive me for saying this, but you remind me of the woman I thought she was. I suppose that sounds bizarre."

"A little." Beth couldn't resist teasing him. It was something she never got to do in her regular life, flirt with an A-list Hollywood director. "Considering you never met me before this weekend."

"You just seem—familiar." His voice was low, his gaze caressing. Oh, he was a potent man. "Like maybe we knew each other in another life."

She held his gaze and felt alone with him on the red carpet, even though crowds of people thronged the rope-lined walkway and more celebrities followed behind. The flashing cameras sparked in her periphery, but her vision, her every sense was filled with him: his carved face, his delicately sculpted lips, his knowing eyes.

A door opened to a possible future. One she'd never anticipated or dreamed, but which could become real if she chose to go through it.

She supposed such doors opened all the time, and which one you entered charted your path beyond. For a moment, she tried to imagine it: a life in Los Angeles, a world of fantasy in the business of creating fantasies. A world next to the spotlight, the partner of a famous man, a world where one's wealth and power and influence all rested on the ability to please, and on what other people thought. He was fascinating, and sexy, and life with him would never be boring or predictable.

Beth looked back at Barony. He was watching her, and when he caught her eye, he winked. He nodded his head toward Regan and lifted his eyebrows in a gleeful *look at me!* expression. Beth laughed out loud. She'd made her choice long ago. Barony was her past, present, and future, and the life she shared with him was the life she would keep choosing, with fresh gratitude and curiosity and commitment, each and every day.

"I have to go rescue my husband," Beth said, and released Timothy's arm.

At least, she hoped he wanted to be rescued.

She let herself enjoy the evening, watching all the movie stars in action, eating an incredible meal and listening to the various speeches as awards were given out. It was like a very expensive end-of-the-year party at her school, but in a different professional world. Regan glowed at the podium as she accepted her award, taking a deep breath to compose herself for her speech.

"I would never have made this film if it weren't for Beth Barony," Regan said. She looked back at their table, and Beth sat up straight as every eye in the room turned toward her. She kept her lips closed when she smiled in case she had seeds in her teeth.

"I met Beth when I was at a very low emotional point," Regan said, "and she helped me turn things around. She's a terrific teacher, and through her eyes, I learned lessons I'll always remember. I really think she saved my life. Thank you, Beth."

Cameras flashed in her direction. Beth knew they would catch every flaw, whatever might be stuck in her teeth, along with the tears dripping down her face. She hoped Tamara had used waterproof mascara, but in truth she didn't care. She clapped and sobbed though the smile on her face went on for miles. Regan Forrester had saved *her* life, and she'd say so to anyone who asked.

After drinking too much and dancing till she had blisters, Beth let out a huge sigh of relief when she finally crawled into bed that night next to Barony. They'd splurged on an expensive hotel room, and the entire suite was more luxurious than anything Beth had ever known.

The bed welcomed her like a cushion of clouds, and the sheets were a heavenly caress. But best of all was Barony's arm snaking around her, his eyes giving her that sleepy, seductive look he wore when he wanted to make love.

Beth wriggled close. "What are these, satin sheets? They feel amazing."

"Egyptian cotton, eight hundred thread count. We should get some for our bed." He nuzzled the hair above her ear.

Beth flung a leg over his hip. "I suppose, since you've been hanging around gorgeous movie stars lately, I'm going to have to up my game."

She meant to sound joking, but a small shred of anxiety surfaced in her voice. Regan Forrester had injected a shot of vitality into nearly every part of Beth's life. She felt reinvigorated as a teacher, her relationships with her kids and friends were closer than ever, her wardrobe had undergone an amazing transformation without too crushing a blow to her credit card. And Barony had been paying a lot more attention.

"What's wrong with our game?" He stroked her leg, down then back up, sliding his fingers beneath the silky negligee she'd bought specially for their LA trip.

"I just thought—maybe you miss the early days. Or my birthday, when we—you know."

He raised an eyebrow. She loved that smirk. It contained the boy she'd met, the young man she'd married, the mature man she'd built her life with and around. Her one great love, now and always.

"Right, your mid-life crisis." He laughed and rolled onto his back, pulling her on top of him. "That was fun, wasn't it?"

Beth's stomach sank. "Do you—miss it?"

"Miss what?"

His hands stroked her back, arousing and calming at the same time. "Wife, you can get wild with me any time you want." He waggled his brows. "But I like—us."

"Boring, old, normal us?" Beth whispered, stretching to kiss his neck.

"Mmm-hmm." She felt the rumble of his voice against her cheek and closed her eyes at the familiar, comfortable, welcome heat. Barony, so solid, so dependable, so predictable. So *hers*.

"Us is good." He pulled back to look at her, a flicker of worry passing through his eyes. "Right?"

"Oh, yes." Beth cupped his face in her hands and smiled. "Us is *great*. I wouldn't trade this for the world."

And she wouldn't, not ever again.

ABOUT THE AUTHOR

Misty Urban is the author of three short story collections and assorted medieval scholarship on the topic of monstrous and misbehaving women. In her historical fiction and romances, she likes to reward her ambitious, rule-breaking heroines with handsome heroes and happy futures. She lives in Iowa with a handsome park ranger, two other budding authors, and a rather heavy collection of books. Find her online at mistyurban.net.

CPSIA information can be obtained
at www.ICGtesting.com
Printed in the USA
LVHW081108080723
751746LV00003B/147

9 781736 224724